Eight Dates and Nights

D0562420

Eight Dates and Nights

SHALOM Y'ALL

BETSY ALDREDGE

Underlined

This is a work of fiction. Names, characters, places, and incidents either are the product of the author's imagination or are used fictitiously. Any resemblance to actual persons, living or dead, events, or locales is entirely coincidental.

Text copyright © 2023 by Betsy Aldredge
Cover art copyright © 2023 by Farjana Yasmin

All rights reserved. Published in the United States by Underlined, an imprint of Random House Children's Books, a division of Penguin Random House LLC, New York.

Underlined is a registered trademark and the colophon is a trademark of Penguin Random House LLC.

GetUnderlined.com

Educators and librarians, for a variety of teaching tools, visit us at RHTeachersLibrarians.com

Library of Congress Cataloging-in-Publication Data is available upon request.
ISBN 978-0-593-71033-3 (trade pbk.) — ISBN 978-0-593-71034-0 (ebook)

The text of this book is set in 12-point Adobe Garamond Pro.
Interior design by Megan Shortt

Printed in the United States of America
1st Printing
First Edition

Random House Children's Books supports the First Amendment and celebrates the right to read.

Penguin Random House LLC supports copyright. Copyright fuels creativity, encourages diverse voices, promotes free speech, and creates a vibrant culture. Thank you for buying an authorized edition of this book and for complying with copyright laws by not reproducing, scanning, or distributing any part in any form without permission. You are supporting writers and allowing Penguin Random House to publish books for every reader.

For my parents,
who let me read whatever I wanted, wherever I wanted,
whether it was socially appropriate or not.

And for Marcus,
my favorite Texas tour guide and partner in all things.
You're my sour cream.

The Christmas season may be magical and delightful
to some, but you could never tell from my gate at LaGuardia
Airport. Clearly, the toddler screaming her head off next to
me agrees. Zero delight there.

Her mom hands her a big red paper cup with a straw
before digging through her ginormous diaper bag while also
juggling a baby. Nearby, a random guy in a Santa suit who
looks like he has had one too many lets out a couple of *ho, ho,*
ho's, followed by a loud belch.

That's when my years of babysitting and being a camp
counselor kick into high gear. I'm not overly fond of most
adults, but I love kids. I always have. I'm pretty sure I even
want to be an elementary school teacher in the future. However, I love kids much more when they aren't crying at a high
pitch directly next to my ear.

"Do you need some help?" I ask the mom, holding out my hand for the toddler. Under normal circumstances, the mom probably wouldn't take help from a stranger, but at this point the toddler is wailing and the drunk Santa is kind of wobbling toward her. He's hopefully friendly, not creepy, but baby girl isn't having it. At all. And neither am I, to be honest.

In contrast, at five two with my curly brown hair, baby face, leggings, and fuzzy Uggs, I hardly look dangerous or overwhelming to the pre–elementary school demographic, or their parents.

"Yes, please! Whatever you can do! Emma, honey," she says over the sobbing, "this nice girl wants to say hello."

I crouch down next to her. "Hi, Emma! I'm Hannah. Do you like dogs or cats?" I ask.

The distraction works, and she stops crying at once.

"Kitty?" she asks, grabbing my hand. Her fine blond pigtails are askew, and her face is as red as her cup.

Her mom flashes me a grateful smile as I sit down in a chair and pull the girl into my lap and pull out my phone to scroll through some cat videos. A couple of seconds of watching cats dressed in Halloween costumes and she's calm but hiccupping now that she's no longer crying. The baby in the mom's arms has fallen asleep as well. Even Way-Too-Jolly St. Nick seems to be sitting down, which is probably a good idea.

I smile briefly. As I do, I realize it's the first real grin to take up residence on my face since finding out I have to go to Texas. Not Austin, or Houston, or anywhere remotely cool.

Nope. I have to go to the middle-of-nowhere East Texas. Population 2,000. Plus me. That makes it 2,001 for the four miserable days I will be there. That would be bad enough, except it's during Hanukkah and I'm being shipped off to see my grandmother. Alone. Not my choice, but my parents don't exactly get along with Nana, so I have to take one for the team, and in this case, it's my family, aka Team Levin.

Last year my brother went. Now it's my turn because my brother is in college and he used some sort of flimsy excuse to get out of it like an internship or studying for the LSAT or whatever. Either way, it worked for him and landed me at the overcrowded gate of the overcrowded airport waiting for a flight that's already been delayed twice and will most likely also be over capacity.

But, for the moment, I push the feeling of dread aside. I'm the child whisperer extraordinaire. Other passengers waiting for the plane are coming over to congratulate me. They don't like crying babies either. The mom is handing me a Starbucks gift card to thank me. Her tired eyes are grateful for the one moment of peace I've managed to give her. As my mom likes to say, "Mitzvah goreret mitzvah," or "one commandment or good deed brings around another." It's kind of a Jewish idea of karma, do one good deed and then someone else will do a good deed, and so on. In this case, in the form of a Starbucks card, which I pocket for later.

The cloying Christmas music is swelling in the airport around me as tinsel on a fake tree waves in the breeze of the air-conditioning. Despite the noise and crowds, it's actually pretty, for a moment.

Maybe it's a sign that things won't be that bad in Texas. Maybe I'll charm my grandmother and my allergies won't even kick in around the horses. Maybe she'll tell me embarrassing stories I can use to taunt my dad for years to come. The doubts creep in, but I choose to ignore them. Until the little girl turns toward me, her eyes widening, her face reddening as her mouth opens wide and she wiggles off my lap and starts to go toward her mom, who is looking in the opposite direction. I think Emma's going to start howling again, so I lean over, but as I do, she toddles back toward me like a less stable Frankenstein's monster. I reach out to steady her, but it's too late. The lid goes flying off her drink, which ends up spilling all over me like a thick shampoo.

Remnants of some sort of kiddie hot cocoa with whipped cream and peppermint topping are now covering my shirt like glittery, warm slime. I let out a shriek as the liquid drips down my front, right into my bra.

I must have startled drunk Santa behind me because he stands up too quickly and trips over someone's luggage. I try to duck, but Emma's in the way and before I know it, yup. Worst-case scenario. I'm on the sticky floor of the airport. On my butt. On what looks like a puddle of beer.

"It's beginning to look a lot like Christmas," someone says under their breath, chuckling.

Crap. It sure is.

Just like in one of those fast-forward time-lapse videos,

everything starts moving really quickly. The mom is absolutely horrified and grabs Emma, who cries again because she wants to stay with me. Other passengers scurry away after handing the mom and me bottles of water, napkins, wet wipes, and everything else they could possibly think of, other than my dignity. That's long, long gone.

The damage is done. Of course, of course, my luggage is checked because it was too big to fit overhead. I only have my backpack and don't have any clothes in it. I could run and buy a new shirt from the newsstand or a gift shop, but that's when they start calling passengers. From here, I can see the line at the store is long as people scramble to buy magazines, gum, and snacks. Too long. I'll never make it there and back in time, and the last thing I want to do is wait for another flight.

As if to take pity on me, a grandmotherly woman digs into her own carry-on and pulls out a red-and-green sweater and hands it over. "Please, take this. I have another one packed. It will be my Christmas gift to you."

Her eyes twinkle over her small Mrs. Claus–like glasses, and I thank her multiple times. That is, until I unfold it and see the monstrosity in front of me. It's an itchy-looking bright green top with plastic bulbs hanging from a moose's antlers. It's 3D. It's practically flammable. And there's no way I'm wearing it. Except for the fact that it's this or my stained shirt for the three-hour-plus flight.

But I don't manage to get any of this across. All I can squeak out is "Thank you! But I'm Jewish!"

"Oh, that's okay, sweetie." That's when she points out what

I missed at the very bottom of the sweater. It's a teeny-tiny menorah. Only it has five candles, so not a menorah at all. It's a candleholder held by the moose, or it's a reindeer hiding behind the moose. Moreover, I doubt the moose is even Jewish. The person who designed it definitely is not. I don't know if it's an oversight or a harbinger of things to come. All I know is that it's going to be a long, humiliating flight.

I go to thank her again, because I'm polite, and also because with my luck, this is all one big prank that's being recorded and I don't want to look like a brat on YouTube and ruin my chances of getting into a good college and finding a job in the future.

So I run to the bathroom and wipe off my bra under my shirt with paper towels, changing into the sweater without even getting to the stall first, because, yeah, the line is long there, too, and it's so quick it's not like anyone even notices.

Once I leave the bathroom, I take a Snap with a frown and send it to my best friends, Abby and Becky, with a crying emoji, which they respond to right away.

LOL, you're never going to meet a cute cowboy in that, Abby writes, not surprising due to her recent fascination with her mom's romance novels.

Then from Becky: *Forget cowboys. Text us the minute you hear about any college. Books before bros . . .* I give her a thumbs-up, send heart emojis to them both, and then shut my phone off, after refreshing my inbox one more time. Nope, no word from any of the schools I applied to, not that I expected to hear so soon.

When I get back to the gate, I look for the woman to thank her again, but then I hear my name being called over the loudspeaker. "Passenger Hannah Levin, please come to the check-in desk. Paging Hannah Levin . . . Report to the check-in area, please."

I duck my head and walk over to the desk, cheeks burning bright red, so that they now match the decorations on the sweater and the cup that was dumped on me. The very put-together airline employee glances at me, her eyebrow raised a bit. Considering her impeccable appearance, *she* has clearly never been seen in public covered in a 3D moose and smelling like I do.

"Am I in trouble?" I croak out. Can they kick me off the flight for smelling like beer or something else? Being an unaccompanied minor? For a second I'm even hopeful I'll be sent home.

She tilts her head. "No, sweetie. We actually have to ask you a favor. Would you mind switching seats so a family could sit together?"

This is the second time in five minutes I've been called sweetie even though sweet is the last thing I am feeling. I sigh but grab the boarding pass she's offering me. It's my second mitzvah of the day. Not bad for a completely crappy day. I'm only hoping this one doesn't end as poorly, considering it involves switching my comfortable window seat in the front of the plane for a cramped spot in the back, right by the bathroom.

I may be grumpy and cynical and my own family may

have sent me off for the week, but that doesn't mean someone else's family should be separated and unhappy during the holidays.

And that's how I end up in a middle seat right in front of Santa and right behind the toddler, who is now fast asleep in clean pajamas because *her* mom was smart enough to pack an extra pair, unlike me. On either side of me is an arguing twentysomething couple who clearly doesn't mind being separated for the duration of the flight, although they keep making passive-aggressive comments to each other about who was supposed to do the Christmas shopping for his parents along with a whole lot of other holiday-related issues. *Ouch.* For the record, I'm Team Hillary because Scott absolutely should have asked her before inviting his ex-girlfriend over for New Year's. Seriously, Scott?

After figuring out the television on my seat isn't working either, I close my eyes, willing myself to nap as well, but soon I'm opening them because I'm too itchy from the sweater to sleep. Hives are forming on the back of my neck and on my arms. Also, music is on full blast on someone's iPad around me.

"Headphones," I mumble. "Get some headphones," I say a little louder as I gulp down some Benadryl for the rash, which is threatening to spread.

Happy Hanukkah to me.

When I get off the plane, my grandmother is waiting for me in jeans, cowboy boots, and a tucked-in green flannel shirt. She's clearly still in great shape from all the work around the ranch, but her hair is grayer. Her wrinkles are more pronounced than the last time I saw her a few years ago, especially her worry lines, which crinkle between her eyebrows when she looks for me in the crowd.

Even in Texas, she stands out in the diverse bunch of people wearing sneakers, business wear, and other more contemporary clothes like hoodies and sweatpants. Yet, somehow it works for her. She looks more comfortable in her clothes than I feel right now, that's for sure.

She smiles at me, but it's a shy smile, like she's not positive if it's actually me. I have grown several inches, in many places, and traded in my sparkly unicorn-and-rainbow-themed clothing, so I don't exactly blame her. And then there's the matter of my completely bizarre sweater. The Hannah she knows wouldn't wear it. Of course, neither would the Hannah I know, yet that's what I'm wearing to see my grandmother for the first time in forever. At least, it feels like forever.

She takes a look at it and bites her lip like she's trying to decide what to say. "You got so tall. And I like your hair like that." She nods once at my grown-out bangs like she's done talking or she's just run out of things to say in the first thirty seconds of our reunion, which doesn't bode well for the next four days.

I look down at my sweater and blush as she finally takes in the full scope of the design.

She lets out a nervous laugh. "Well, this outfit is un-expected. I mean, it's very spirited. I just wouldn't think it was your style. I remember you didn't really enjoy standing out so much."

I blow a curl out of my face because my arms are full with my coat and my backpack. "Oh, yeah. It's not mine. Still a practicing Jew. Not that there's anything wrong with celebrating Christmas. . . . Millions of people do. . . . So don't report me to that elf if you have one on a shelf. . . ." I trail off, not wanting to offend her within the first three minutes of seeing her in several years. My grandmother wasn't born Jewish, al-though my grandpa Mel was, but neither of them were partic-ularly religious. As a consequence, my dad grew up in a fairly secular home. He became more observant once he moved to New York, met my mom, and had us, from what I gather.

"Anyway, it's kind of a long story that involves a good deed that didn't end so well." I shudder, still getting over that hot chocolate bath.

I take the opportunity to stretch my neck and shoulders after being stuck in that small middle seat, only here I feel cramped into my grandmother's idea of me from ten years ago versus the person I am now. What if she doesn't like who I've become? For all intents and purposes, she barely knows me.

She holds out her hand for my backpack, which I hand over to her. "It's heavy," I say, not mentioning that it's mostly full of books and electronics since I'm anticipating being bored, stuck in the middle of nowhere for the next four days. As I hand it over, my back feels better already.

"No heavier than a saddle," she says with a similar shrug that I recognize as one my dad often gives. Which reminds me to text my parents that I've arrived and that I'm with Nana.

I guess some things are family traits, not that my dad, the buttoned-up, city-loving professor, would admit he had much in common with his earthy, outdoorsy mom. Yet, he was one of the two people who insisted I head here before our traditional family Hanukkah celebration. The other was my mom. She is normally very respectful of her mother-in-law, at least in front of me, but that doesn't mean she had any desire to join me here either. Nope. I'm all alone with my resentment for four days.

Without another word, I follow my grandmother through the busy airport decorated in Christmas trees, giant ornaments, lights, and blow-up snowmen, past the unfamiliar fast-food stands for shrimp and pork places that are extremely non-kosher. Just like the vast majority of decorations other than the small, sad menorah that is on top of the counter of the bakery. I count the candles and yep. At least it's a "real" menorah, unlike the one on my sweater. I can't stand how Hanukkah is commercialized and lumped in with Christmas, but at the moment, I'm too light-headed and tired to care. My stomach rumbles, surprising me because I didn't expect to be so hungry after the whole trauma on the plane. It must be louder than I thought because my grandmother turns and frowns at me. "Are you hungry?"

"Yeah. I didn't eat much today."

"Do you see anything you can eat?" she asks, gesturing around the food court area. She doesn't quite get my eating habits. While I'm not a hundred percent kosher, I do try to eat kosher style most of the time, i.e., no pork or shellfish, no mixing meat and dairy. I'm not as strict as my mom, who grew up Conservative, since I grew up attending a Reform synagogue, but I try to be mindful of what I eat, something that's probably going to be harder away from a major city.

I debate the merits of airport sushi before my stomach flips, and I mumble something about grabbing Starbucks. A few minutes later, sugary latte and lousy bagel in hand, thanks to the gift card from Emma's mom, I am feeling better, especially when my luggage shows up. I almost cry with relief as I pull the purple rolling bag off the carousel and open it right there to pull out a clean shirt and be done with my itchy, ugly sweater.

But as I do, something's wrong. It's not my bag at all! In my hand I'm holding someone else's clothes. And worse, to my absolute mortification, I'm holding on to someone's black-and-red-fur-trimmed holiday-themed nightie over my head. I gasp loudly, turning the color of that fur trim as Hillary, the twentysomething woman who had been sitting next to me on the plane, runs over to pull it out of my hand and stuff it back into the suitcase.

"I've never seen that before. Did you get that from someone else?" Her boyfriend, Scott, scowls at her and speaks loud enough that everyone around us can hear.

"It was supposed to be a surprise! From Santa!" she says, pulling it back out of the suitcase and throwing it on the ground.

"I'm s-so sorry!" I blush as Hillary and her boyfriend get into yet another fight. This one is my fault, and my grandmother starts laughing and can't stop, which only makes it worse. Ugh, if this is what dating is, count me out of that whole thing. No way, no thank you. Love is clearly overrated and messy, and while I may be Jewish, I *know* that it was not Santa's fault at all. It was brewing a long time and no pack of reindeer could fix this mess.

When the girl and her boyfriend finally roll the bag out of sight, leaving a puddle of inappropriate jingle-belled clothing behind them, and my grandmother wipes her eyes and catches her breath, it hits me. All the luggage is off the plane. Mine isn't there at all. The carousel goes around and around, empty.

I run from carousel to carousel all up and down the terminal to see if mine ended up on the wrong one, but it's useless. My luggage was smart enough to say "Nope, not going there." I only wish I was that smart.

Finally, I manage to find an open window at the luggage counter, but considering the noncommittal response from the employee, I'm not hopeful that my luggage will make it here before I need to leave to go back to New York.

I'm also not hopeful the couple will make it to New Year's, but that I can't help. I have enough issues of my own at the moment.

"You have to admit, it's a little funny," my grandmother says with a twinkle in her eye, craning her neck to see if the couple is still in sight.

They must not be, because she turns back toward me.

I'm having a hard time finding the humor in it. I try to swallow down the past few hours of the lousy flight and lost luggage and put on a brave face as my grandmother talks about her horses on the ranch. Based on her relaxed chatter, it's like the lingerie episode broke a spell, at least for her.

I'm more wary. Not just of her, but of the next four days in general.

Soon, we're in her truck, without my suitcase but with what she calls "a good story to tell everyone in town." Seeing as how the town is pretty small, it shouldn't take long, I say, but she just laughs. "It can take a whole hour to get through the general store when you just go in for two things. One thing about Rosenblum is that people looove to talk and no one is in a rush. I think you'll like it."

"Strangers making small talk? Um, hard pass . . . ," I say under my breath.

As she relaxes, my grandmother's Texan accent becomes thicker, her words slower and more drawled out and musical. It's a stark contrast to the fast-paced, excitable voices I'm used to in New York. That's when I realize that my dad's either lost most of his accent or works hard to conceal it and wonder if it's one of the things that causes tension between him and my nana.

I bite my lip to stop myself from asking and instead try to pay attention to the conversation, stifling a yawn. "That's pretty much the opposite of New York. Everyone is in a rush because there's so much to do and so many places to go. We even have a word for it: FOMO. It means 'fear of missing out.'"

I frown because it's exactly what I'm feeling right now. My folks, Abby and Becky, everybody back home is having more fun than I am this break. As if to reiterate the point, a text comes in from Abby with a picture of her and Becky and a couple of other kids from our school ice skating at Bryant Park. Abby is smiling, holding a hot chocolate, her brown hair flying in her face. Becky's nose is red from the cold and ice seems to be forming on her long, curly hair and on her mittens, and yet they seem happy. I can't help it. I envy them both.

Miss you! Xoxo

I text back a sad emoji until Abby sends one with a cowboy hat and a heart and the Texas flag.

Send pics, Becky writes.

Ooh! Maybe you'll meet a lumberjack! My mom has a romance book with a hot lumberjack. I mean, if there are no cowboys available.

I type back. *A, I think there are more lumberjacks in the Pacific Northwest, and B, I think anyone I meet in Rosenblum will be over 80 years old. Not anyone you want to spend time with over a roaring fire . . .*

I look out my window for something to photograph, but it's just one giant strip mall in between Houston and whatever town we're in. Every Target looks the same. There's nothing interesting or even ironically funny, so I put my phone away.

"This place is pretty popular," Nana says as she pulls into a Whataburger drive-through. Whataburger is one of my brother Josh's absolute favorite things about Texas. He's less kosher than I am and swears their burgers are better than Shake Shack or any other chain, but the heavy, subpar bagel is still sitting in my stomach like lead and apprehension, so I just ask for a soda.

Nana balances her burger and drink expertly as she pulls out of the parking lot and back on the endless highway. She doesn't have the GPS on, so I don't know where we are, but eventually I must have fallen asleep thanks to the gentle rumble of the truck and the lack of annoying passengers arguing around me.

I awake with a start as we pull into a parking space on

what appears to be the main street of her town, Rosenblum, founded 1868, according to the sign. Only, it looks different from the last time I saw it. It's still small, but seems more like a re-creation of a small town at a theme park than the slightly dusty, run-down version I remembered. The buildings on one side of the street appear newly painted white, pink, green, and blue with old-fashioned iron or wooden signs swinging from the wraparound awning that joins them. Benches and porch swings and rocking chairs sit in front of many of the stores. The other side also features wooden buildings, but they are separated from each other and have more traditional signs above.

"Nana, where's the movie theater where we saw *Frozen*?"

It had to be maybe the last time my parents, Josh, and I were all here in Texas together at the same time.

"Oh, honey, it closed. There's a big antique store there now. See? We get some weekenders coming up, so there are more tourists, but not enough to support a movie theater. Actually, a lot of the businesses have been struggling. Or the owners retire and their kids don't want to move back here, so they sell or close. It's sad, really."

I turn all around the street and see what she means. Gone is the candy store/pharmacy, which used to make their own fountain sodas. In its place is what looks like a salon. As a New Yorker, I know neighborhoods change a lot over time. Every year restaurants close and inevitably a new pharmacy will move into that space, or something else that we don't need. I also know that longtime residents and businesses are often pushed out, but I guess I didn't expect it to happen here. I don't say it to my grandmother, but I get it. My dad did the same thing, moved away for college and never came back for more than a short visit.

But when I glance at the old theater where I had such happy memories, my eyes well up a little. I never thought about what happens to a town when people move away.

My grandmother walks toward the general store, and I dab at my eyes. I'm really hoping it's not going to be one of those hour-long conversations, but that's when I see him.

There's a boy, probably about my age. He's tall and lanky with longish, wavy dark brown hair and long limbs that remind me of a baby giraffe, cute but kind of awkward, like he hasn't grown into himself yet. He's got a goofy look to him, especially considering he's dressed like a giant hot dog and holding a tray of something, passing out samples with a big grin.

Finally, I have something to take a photo of, so I Snapchat my friends right away.

Lumberjacks, 0. Hot dogs, 1.

I don't know, he's pretty cute for deli meat. Add ketchup and some plaid and totally the same, Abby writes back.

Relish him! Becky writes, followed by a series of emojis that starts getting out of control.

I shake my head before following my grandmother into the general store, which is mostly a hardware store, but, Nana has told me, also carries stuff for horses, birds, and barn cats, and antacids, too. I'm looking at sunglasses on a display next to hot sauces when hot-dog guy turns toward the window and gives me a little wave that makes me feel slightly mean for joking about him with my friends.

There's no way he could have seen my screen or known that I was talking about him, and yet, I hide my head, shielding my guilty face for a second. But he doesn't look mad, rather he looks intrigued. Or as intrigued as a hot dog can possibly look.

I'm confused as to why this strange guy would wave, but maybe it's a friendly Texan thing. As a New Yorker, I'm taught to be naturally suspicious of anyone being friendly, because they usually want me to join a cult or go to a comedy club or something. Since I'm not in New York anymore, I give a small wave back, until he looks even more confused. I turn around and see he's actually waving at the middle-aged guy behind me.

Great. Now I've humiliated myself in front of a guy wearing a hot-dog costume. I didn't think it was possible, but yeah, it's a new low in a day that has already had a couple of Grand Canyon–sized lows. I'm officially more embarrassing than a guy dressed as meat on a bun. He's still smiling while I'm most certainly not. I duck behind some duck-hunting hats. The irony is not lost on me.

Unfortunately, the camouflage doesn't work because that's where I am when my grandmother finds me. She starts loading my arms with various feeds—horse feed, dog food, bird food, and cat food—while I try to keep my head down. This is why I don't wave at strangers or talk to them.

My grandmother, on the other hand, is still talking to the

clerk when she introduces me. "Nancy, this is Hannah, my granddaughter. She came to spend part of her break with me, isn't that nice?"

"Oh, Christmas break with your grandmother, how special!" Nancy says.

I wince, but don't correct her that it's a winter break, not a Christmas break. I'm used to all the winter holidays being lumped in together, but it's somehow harder here, where I'm the only one who notices.

"Oh, yes! I imagine it will be good for you to have some help around the ranch. Miss Hannah, how do you feel about mucking out the stalls? I bet Santa will bring you something nice for that . . . ," Nancy says while ringing up my grandmother.

My grandmother nods politely and finishes chitchatting, not correcting her that I don't celebrate Christmas.

My face probably registers exactly how I feel about having to pass as a non-Jew because Nancy and my grandmother start laughing, misinterpreting my displeasure. "Oh, don't worry, honey," my grandmother says, "I'll find you something else to wear to clean out the stalls. Don't want to get that sweater dirty. I don't know if it's machine washable."

She doesn't get that my horrified face has more to do with her hiding that I'm Jewish, not to mention spending my vacation working. Suddenly my pile of books and my downloaded music seem like a distant and overly optimistic memory.

It's been only a day, and I already miss New York, where you can walk around in a unicorn onesie singing show tunes and no one will say anything. They're all too busy doing their own thing. Even hot-dog guy wouldn't get a second glance in New York, where weird is ordinary. You have to be a whole lot weirder than hot-dog guy to get noticed, and I miss that. And in New York, people also don't assume that everyone is the same. If I were there, I would have no problem correcting the hardware store lady and telling her I'm Jewish, but here, I don't know what I'm supposed to do. I don't want to make my grandmother uncomfortable, but I shouldn't feel bad of something I'm actually proud of.

My unasked question is why she, who was married to someone Jewish for fifty years and had Jewish children, would feel the need to hide it. Is there something I'm missing? Remembering my parents reminding me to be polite and respectful to my grandmother, I let it go. For now. I can put up with anything for four days, but it goes in the column of Reasons I Don't Want to Come Back.

As we walk out and put the bags into the trunk, I take one more quick glance behind me, just in time to see hot-dog guy try to squeeze himself into the small door of a storefront before eventually giving up and waddling around the back of the building. Based on the slump of his shoulders and how many samples are still on his tray, it looks like I'm not the only one having a day that is not filled with much to relish at all.

3

The needlepoint sheep are the first reminder I'm no longer in my room in our New York City apartment. I wake up and look around Nana's guest room. It's a little old-fashioned and rustic, but charming, I guess, although not exactly my style. The bed has a blue-and-white quilt with a circle pattern that echoes the watercolor painting of bluebonnets, a Texas wildflower, on the wall. There's one chair, an antique wash-stand with a pitcher and a bowl, a small chest of drawers with a lamp on it, and spotty Wi-Fi.

Sighing, I step onto the braided rug and the wooden floor creaks loudly, but I don't worry about waking up my grand-mother. She's probably been up for hours. So I make my way downstairs in her borrowed plaid pajamas, which are just a little too big on me, but soft. She must have a whole wardrobe of plaid flannel, but I'm not complaining. I even borrowed some of my dad's flannels from the nineties—and by borrowed, I mean took with no intention of giving back, not that he minded. My mom was thrilled for him to dress like more of an adult, too.

A huge spread covers the round wooden farm table in the kitchen. Another change from my regular routine. At home our usual is oatmeal or cold cereal. Maybe a granola bar if we're in a rush.

The rooster clock tells me it's only seven o'clock, which means it's eight in New York, where I've never seen a rooster, real or even depicted on a clock. In fact, I'm still pondering why they would be considered attractive decor in the first place as my grandmother serves my breakfast.

"Thanks, Nana. You didn't have to do all this," I say, taking a huge bite of a blueberry pancake as soon as it hits my plate. Yum. Much better than oatmeal, although I'd trade it in a second to be back home, where I can just get a bagel from a coffee cart.

"I wanted to. It's not every day my favorite granddaughter comes to visit," my grandmother says, pouring some syrup on her own stack.

She chews quietly, but what comes through loud and clear is the reminder that I haven't made enough of an effort to see her or stay connected beyond occasionally saying hello when my dad puts me on the phone with her. As if sensing the tension, she puts down her napkin and offers me a tight smile. "I thought we'd go outside and see the horses a bit later."

Right, horses. Huge, intimidating beasts. They're beautiful, but there's something too otherworldly and intuitive about them. They know too much. I like my animals to be smaller and not as smart as I am. Cats and dogs I can handle, but I'm not sure about horses. However, I'm here and I don't want to disappoint her again. After all, I promised my parents I would spend quality time with her and be the perfect granddaughter, just like I have to be the perfect daughter all the time, too.

So after I eat and help my grandmother clean up, I get dressed in my own clothes, which she's washed, and then I find myself in the barn, full of antihistamines. Now it's just me, two giant brown horses, a shovel, and a wheelbarrow.

I rub at my slightly itchy eyes and then mumble to myself as the country music station in the background, which my grandmother keeps on for the horses and the barn cats, plays twangy versions of holiday songs, not a Hanukkah one in the mix. I guess the horses aren't Jewish either, or the radio hosts, for that matter.

Of course, that's when Josh FaceTimes me from his dorm room at Brandeis, where he's staying over the holiday break.

In my rush to answer the phone, I somehow manage to wipe my forehead with my work glove that's covered in dirt, or worse. To be honest, I don't want to know.

"Hello?" I ask, moving the phone in multiple directions before finding a spot with the best signal. I put the phone down on a ledge and grunt in exertion, trying to breathe in and out of my mouth rather than my nose. Horses may be pretty, but their stalls don't smell great, something I wish I didn't know firsthand. They are much cleaner and more fragrant on Netflix shows about cowboys.

"Just checking in," he says, moving some sweatshirts off his bed.

"I'm out in the barn."

"Is that a new farm to table restaurant?" he jokes as I put a big pile of horse manure in the wheelbarrow and glare at him.

"No, it's apparently where you send little sisters when you're an evil mastermind and never *ever* want to get another Hanukkah gift again."

Josh winces.

"Oh, and you're lucky they haven't invented scratch-and-sniff phone screens yet."

"How are Paul and Ringo? Can I see them? I just want to say hi, see if they remember me."

"Who?" I ask.

"The horses. They're named after the Beatles. Nana loves the Beatles. She had Georgie, who was a mare, John, and Yoko, too, for a while. Georgie passed away, but John and Yoko didn't get along with the others, so she sold them to a neighbor after they broke up the group. Go figure."

"I didn't know that. Dad always played the Beatles for us when we were kids," I say. "I guess that's why. . . ." Memories of my dad plucking out "Here Comes the Sun" in my bedroom when I was little flood over me. I gulp back that emotion when I realize what Josh is implying.

"Oh, and it's not Yoko's fault the band broke up. That's total misogynist crap. Lots of bands break up! It happens all the time. John wanted to go in a different direction musically. It coincided with artistic stuff he was doing with Yoko, but it wasn't her fault."

"I guess you do listen to Dad," Josh interrupts. "Because that's his argument, too, but back to the more important point. You don't know the horses' names because you never asked about them, or bothered to find out what Nana likes," he says with a meaningful look and the soft voice he's always used to calm me down, something he's been good at for ages and takes very seriously.

"It's good that you're down there to spend time with Nana. To get to know her. Before it's too late. It's not like our grandmother is getting any younger."

I hate when he's right, which is why I normally don't concede so easily.

"It goes both ways, Josh," I say. "If she bothered to get to know me, she'd know I have zero desire to be out here when I could be, um, I don't know, bingeing *Stranger Things* again, watching random BookToks, reading fantasy or sci-fi, who knows? I'd rather do any of that right about now. Don't grandmothers normally want to bake cookies? That I could get excited about! I like cookies. Much more than manual labor."

"Did she make you her famous blueberry pancakes yet?" Josh asks when I'm done complaining.

"Um, yeah," I said sheepishly. It hadn't occurred to me that Josh had experienced them, too. "She made them this morning. They were really good."

"Maybe that's *her* version of cookies. You can bake and chill at home, anyway," he says, ignoring my point entirely. "You're in Texas, get some brisket, ride a tractor, meet a cowboy, experience it all. . . . Have you gone to the general store yet? They have these pecan bars and warm socks that are awesome. . . ."

Before I can respond, I hear a girl's voice giggling in the background. "Study partner?" I ask with an evil grin. He's so busted. Mom and Dad would be far from thrilled if he's hanging out with girls instead of studying for the LSAT. But he just smirks. He's always been able to get away with stuff based on his ability to get people to like him. He's extremely likable and easygoing, both qualities I didn't exactly inherit. I'm "intense" like my mom, according to Josh, which he takes to mean difficult, but I think there's nothing wrong with having opinions and sticking to them. It's called conviction.

"What can I say? I like brilliant women." More giggling in the background before he winks at me as the call starts losing its connection.

"Wait!" I yelp, hoping he can hear me. "How do I get the smell of horse manure out of my hair?"

I can just barely hear him laugh before the connection is completely lost. He's probably going back to his adoring LSAT tutor, and I'm stuck with a growing pile of horse manure and a stink that I'm not sure can be undone by a simple shower or even three of them back-to-back. And I thought the airport incident was bad. This is so much worse. How is it fair? And if my grandmother wanted to spend time with me, why would *this* be the activity she's chosen? It's not like it's going to make me want to come back to Texas any time soon. If ever.

One of the horses must have heard my kvetching because he sticks his whole head into the stall I'm trying to clean. "Yeah, yeah, I'm working on it. This isn't the Ritz; you have to be patient." But as I say that, he rests his head on the shelf and just looks at me with huge brown eyes that seem to sense my frustration and want to help. If that's even possible.

I put down the shovel, wipe my forehead with the back of my arm this time, and go over to him. "Ringo?" I guess. I reach out a tentative hand for him to sniff. He rubs against my hand and sighs as if content I'm paying attention to him. "Fine, I guess you're pretty cute, or handsome, or whatever. But that still doesn't mean I want to clean up after you. I don't even like cleaning up after myself." But the horse leans over and rests his head on my shoulder. It's heavy, but somehow comforting, and I feel a little less alone.

He gets me, even though some of the people around me don't.

That's how my grandmother finds us when she comes into the barn with a big glass of iced tea for me. "Ah, I see you're making friends with Paul; he's such a flirt. Don't give him any sugar cubes. The vet said they aren't good for him."

"Yeah, but I thought he was Ringo."

"Oh, no, honey, Ringo's the one with the stripe on his face. He's also much bigger than Paulie here and less energetic because he's a little older."

I look over at the other stall, and Ringo does seem more chill, just mindlessly chewing on some hay like he is completely over it. He takes one look at me, then goes back to eating, not impressed. Well, it's mutual, Ringo.

Paul blows out his lips like he's laughing at me. Stupid city girl, he's probably thinking as my grandmother leads him out of his stall and toward a big open space where she hooks him up to leashes on both sides of him before taking a shower-head off the wall and giving him a bath. The horse stomps and throws his head back, but he looks like he doesn't mind so much.

My grandmother's movements are confident and calm as she speaks in a low, reassuring voice to Paul, not unlike how Josh tried to speak to me. It seems to work better on the horse.

When she's done, she dries him off, then hands me a brush. I just look at it for a moment, until she smiles. "Don't worry, he likes it. He has to be nice and clean before his appointment. Do you know that he's a therapy horse? He's great with autistic kids in particular, so I got us certified. The only problem is that he knows he's special. All the handsome boys do." She pets his nose, and he lets out a little neigh. Show-off.

I think about what Josh said and decide to try to make the best of the situation. "So, Nana," I ask while brushing the horse until my grandmother takes the brush from me and corrects my technique, then gives it back, "don't you get lonely out here?"

My grandfather passed about eleven years ago, and since then she's been living alone. I barely remember my grandpa Mel, only my dad being really sad when he died. However, I do know my dad thinks his mother should have moved somewhere else to be closer to family.

"Not really, Hannah, sweetie. I have my horses and my friends. I'm far too busy with the horse therapy to be lonely. Also, there's a difference between being alone and being lonely. Being alone is an opportunity for independence. I spent most of my life taking care of others, and now I get to make my own rules, to try new things. I hope you'll get to do that in college soon. It seems like your brother is."

I stop myself from rolling my eyes, something that annoys my mom to no end. I assume my grandmother would have a similar reaction. So instead, I just give a noncommittal noise and mumble "Yes, ma'am," like my dad said to say in Texas. If my non-answer bothers her, she doesn't say anything.

I am looking forward to college, but unlike my brother, I plan to choose a major right away, stick to it, and graduate early in order to save money for grad school since I know that I want to be an elementary school teacher. I've always been excited about teaching kids to read and to love books the way I do. I've applied to a range of schools—Columbia and NYU, where my dad teaches; a couple of SUNY schools; Penn State; a couple of small liberal arts colleges in New England— all within a four-hour radius by car. I've mapped everything out. At my dad's insistence, I also applied to his alma maters, University of Texas and Rice, but it was only to humor him. I can't imagine going so far away from my parents and my friends. It's not part of my plan.

Lost in thought, I must be doing a lousy job because my grandmother takes the brush from me and puts it away. "I know you probably think it's mean that I made you take care of the horses today, but if you are going to ride them, you need to know how to take care of them and they need to trust you. There's no better way to get to know them, to start the conversation."

She walks Paul over to the wall where the saddles are and puts a blanket on his back.

I stare up at the giant beast. There's no way I can get up on him, and what if I fall? It's a long way down to the ground and an even longer way to the closest hospital. I checked before I got on the plane. It's a twenty-minute drive to a hospital, fifteen minutes to the nearest fire department, and twenty-five minutes to the closest urgent care.

"Nana! I've never been on a horse. Maybe a pony once, but that was a long time ago, when my parents took us to some harvest festival upstate to pick apples. I'm not saying it wasn't nice taking care of Paul. I'm happy to help get him ready for therapy so he can help others. That's a mitzvah, for sure! But I think I'm going to stay on the ground, where it's safe."

"Do you always play it safe?" my grandmother asks as she takes the blanket off and studies me. Maybe it's my imagination, but the horse looks as disappointed as she does.

I hesitate before answering, frowning. I don't know how she's able to read me so well, but I'm not sure I like it.

"Most of the time," I admit, smoothing my hair, which is out of control in the Texas humidity. My hair, like the rest of me, doesn't know what to do in this strange climate, other than act out, whether it's a good idea or not.

4

"I think you've earned a little independence," my grandmother says after we've cleaned up.

I don't know whether she is taking pity on me and wants to give me a break, or if we have already run out of things to talk about, but my grandmother drops me off in town after lunch so that I can get some time to myself. "I'll pick you up in an hour and a half after my book club," she says.

I would ask her about what she's reading, but I actually want the time to myself and reliable Wi-Fi more, so I just say goodbye and head out of the car. Luckily, I'm now in a plain T-shirt and yet another flannel over my leggings, and my Uggs. Nothing to be embarrassed by, as long as I don't do anything ridiculous, or still smell like a stall. I've taken an extralong shower, and at this point, I can't smell myself, so who knows. But assuming there are a lot of horse lovers around here, maybe no one will notice anyway. Or maybe they'll be too polite to say anything if they do notice. That's one thing I've noticed already. People are all about manners here.

I start out in the antique store, but it's in the process of closing up for the day. "You can take a quick peek around, darling," the owner says. "You're Miss Sarah's granddaughter, Hannah, right?"

"Um, yeah, how did you know?" I ask just before I remember I'm supposed to say "Yes, ma'am," so I add that, too, before I look down at myself and wonder if there is some resemblance. My grandmother is slender and tall, but sturdy like my dad with blondish-grayish hair and bluish eyes, where I take after my mom, petite with dark curls and dark eyes.

The woman at the store waves off the question. "I saw her drop you off in her truck, and she had told me last week that you were coming to see her. Pleased as punch she was. I'm Gillian, by the way." Her eyes twinkle from behind her dark-framed glasses. "I've known your grandmother since grade school. Do let me know if you have any questions."

I spend the next few minutes looking at all the antiques, most of which are either too big or too breakable to bring back with me. I see some vintage eighties stuff I think my mom and dad would love, like old tin lunch boxes with Ms. Pac-Man and Care Bears on them, but the shop is closing, so I promise to come back another day.

I think I remember to say thank you as I leave the store and the bell rings behind me. Soon I'm on the sidewalk. The new hair and nail salon doesn't interest me, although my nails are a mess after taking care of the horses. Neither does the cobbler, the fishing gear place, a lawyer, or the bridal store. Nope. Definitely not that one, especially after witnessing the couple next to me on the plane. Eesh. Anyone who says opposites attract should be forced to share a flight with them.

Plus, none of the stores would have Wi-Fi or anywhere to sit. So I keep walking, my hands starting to get cold. I thought Texas would be warmer in December than New York, but the cold air sneaks up every once in a while and nips at me, as if reminding me of my lost luggage full of sweatshirts, plaid lounge pants, and other comfy clothes. I wonder if they miss me as much as I miss them.

A text comes in from my mom with a GIF of some eighties actor saying *I miss you* followed by one from my dad of a dog with sad eyes asking *Whatcha doing?*

I roll my eyes both in real life and in emoji form, and send back a GIF of tumbleweeds blowing down a deserted street and write *Just sightseeing* with a laughing emoji. They send kisses and hearts and more laughter, which makes me smile to myself for a second, before that smile fades.

I'm still annoyed at them, even if I probably miss them even more, especially walking around alone by myself. While my grandmother may prefer solitude, I grew up in a crowded city, in an apartment that was always full of loud people. To me, the noise is lively and energetic. I can barely sleep when it's too quiet, although there's something to be said for the charm of this town, if you're into that picturesque kind of thing where you can see the sky and no one throws trash for the pizza-loving rats on the subway tracks.

I wiggle my toes to warm them up a little. I've only ever been to Texas in the sweltering summer, when you dash from one air-conditioned space to another. Winter is completely different, calmer and more serene.

The storefronts all seem to have Christmas displays with trees, wreaths, elves, and other woodland creatures. It's just like something out of one of those Hallmark movies that Abby's mom loves. But then I look closer across the street from the general store and see blue lights coming from one of the storefronts. The blue lights stand out against all the red, green, and white, so I look again and see that the lights are coming from a menorah and a bunch of dreidels lit up. Dreidels in Rosenblum! Without even thinking about traffic, I walk directly across the street to get a better look.

A car beeps, but it's almost half-hearted. They're not in a rush, and neither am I. There's nowhere else to go.

I stand still in front of the shop and take it all in, as if drawn to the shiny lights, a moth to a flame. No, more like a moth to a menorah.

Blum and Sons Deli. The sign glows in neon red Yiddish-inspired lettering, just like on the Lower East Side of Manhattan. It's such a welcome sight that I first wonder if it's a mirage. I don't remember seeing it before, but the last time I was here I was small and more interested in Disney movies.

Could I be dreaming about Jewish cuisine? Yeah, I absolutely could. To be honest, I've had dreams about my mom's babka before. But in this case, I don't think I am. To be sure, I lean my head against the window for a second, take a deep whiff of something frying coming from the shop, and then open up the door to the mostly empty deli.

It looks similar to Katz's or any of the other old-school places in the city that serve pastrami sandwiches the size of a studio apartment. A big case with schmears of cream cheese, lox, whitefish, knishes, beets, pickles, and spreads line one wall of the place. The refrigerator case has at least a dozen kinds of seltzer, Dr. Brown's, and some other sodas and iced teas. A long counter with red vinyl stools is in the middle of the store. A chalkboard menu hangs overhead. On the other side of the place are small booths with larger tables in the middle. The floor is checkered with black and white tile that is starting to chip like it's seen better days, just like the store.

The average age of the handful of customers looks like it's about eighty, and that's *with* me bringing down the average significantly.

Before looking up at the menu, I check my phone. Yes! It recognizes Wi-Fi in the deli. This magical, Jewish store is also a hot spot. It's like I was meant to find it, just like a fairy-tale cottage hidden in the woods or a wishing well. With a big grin, I sit down at the counter on one of the small round stools and pull out a ridged plastic menu, yellow with age and something that may be a soup stain. It's well loved, which actually gives me confidence in the place. It's not some newfangled concept shop that's just a niche trend or a franchise. It's not trying to reinvent and deconstruct deli food or create some theme-park version of it. I'm pretty sure it's the real deal, a place where people get so excited they spill soup on the menu in the middle of a conversation. Now that I'm here, I'm famished, which might have something to do with the amazing smells coming from the kitchen.

It's only been a day since I left New York, but it reminds me of how accustomed I am to having a community around me, to having tons of people who just get me, not just one lone horse. Coming to Texas has felt like landing on a new planet where everyone speaks the same language but doesn't understand one another. Here, the menu alone speaks to me. It says chopped liver, noodle kugel, and other carbs and meats that have sustained my people for generations. Regardless of where we've lived in the world, we've cooked, we've found common languages like Yiddish. We've adapted and we've longed for what we've left behind. This place speaks to that longing, at least to me, who longs for New York, for my family. And I haven't even had a bite of food yet.

I'm looking at the menu and deciding between potato latkes or blintzes. As much as I love potatoes, the sweet cheese filling and berry topping of the blintz is probably delicious, too. I'm still trying to decide when a boy about my age comes out from the kitchen in a bright blue apron with a menorah on it that says *Ready to Get Lit*.

I can't quite place him until he smiles and walks directly toward me with a swagger I recognize. It's hot-dog guy, and apparently, he's not *just* a hot dog, he's a Hebrew National hot dog, like me. Cute, Jewish, and a purveyor of deli food. It's almost not fair. If I could design a dream boy, it might be him with his perfect cheekbones and full lips and wavy hair that belong in a movie about dukes or other romantic old-timey heroes. Who could resist the temptation? Other than me. I can resist a lot.

"Hey, I know you," he says. "From the general store yesterday."

I blush and look down at the menu. Without the costume, he's adorable, but I'm here for fried potatoes and reliable Wi-Fi, not to flirt with boys, especially boys in my grandmother's small town who I will probably never see again, if I'm lucky.

In four days, this will just be a memory.

"Doesn't ring a bell," I say, biting a lip, suddenly finding their list of appetizers very appetizing indeed. "I mean, I meet a lot of hot dogs." I give him my signature deadpan voice, the one that says I'm not interested in what he's selling. Other than deli food. *That* is of great interest to me.

"Do I need to get my costume on again?" he says. "Because I'd really rather not. It's itchy, if you must know the truth. I should have sprung for the pastrami costume. I think it was organic cotton, unlike the polyester I wore the other day. You live, you learn." He leans on the counter; yeah, either he's overly friendly or he's flirting. It's hard to tell in this place where strangers actually talk to each other for fun on a regular basis.

I look up at him, and he's giving me a sardonic grin.

"No need." I push my hair behind my ear. "Yeah, I was

the weirdo who waved at you, but it was one of those things where I thought you were waving at me and I was just being polite. Let's just say mistakes were made. Won't happen again." I purposefully glance back down and bite my lip to stop myself from smiling at his Texan accent and sincere, wide-eyed expression.

While Abby's mom may have a thing for lumberjacks, it turns out I may have a thing for guys with access to deli food, not that I am going to let myself go there. My stomach may be the way to my heart, but I can feed it myself, thank you very much.

"How about I wave at you now for real, if you'll tell me your name and we can start over?" he says with a lazy grin.

The dude has several different kinds of them, and they are all cute, if you're into that sort of thing, which I'm not because I usually prefer broody to beaming.

"Wait," he says, still smiling, "do you only wave at people in costume? Because I may have other costumes out back. I was a Jedi for Purim, I'll have you know. I slayed." He laughs at his own joke but stops when I just raise an eyebrow.

"Nope. That's fine. I'm good. No costume needed. I'm just visiting," I say. "I'm Hannah," I add, practically as an afterthought.

"Well, Just Visiting Hannah, I'm Noah Blum. And I live here in scenic Rosenblum. In fact, it's even kind of named after us. We used to be Rosenblum. Someone shortened it a couple generations ago. Now we're just Blum. Blum where you're planted! That's the family motto," he says, pointing at the sign on the door. He must be one of the sons in Blum & Sons.

I glance back at the storefront and frown. Something seems off. "Can I ask you a question?"

"Yes, we have the best matzah ball soup in three counties, maybe four if Ira Cohen's finally retired, if that's the question," he says, bringing over a small dish of pickles for me. Little does he know he's speaking my love language. Pickles are one of my favorites. They're all about potential. They start out a cucumber and, by sheer will and patience, transform into something much more complex and tasty. Unlike people, pickles are praised when they become more sour and a little salty. I should have been a pickle. Then I would be appreciated for who I truly am.

I clear my throat but take a pickle. It's chilled and satisfyingly fresh, crunching in half when I bite into it. It's sour, but not too sour, just how I like them.

"Good to know. I hope Ira Cohen has a very nice retirement. However, my question had more to do with the gnome in the window." I gesture with my hand, which has already picked up another pickle, as his eyes follow mine.

"Oh? Mordechai? I've had him for years. No, not really. I think I got him last year from a craft market or something, but he *looks* ancient. What do you want to know about my gnomie? Get it? Like homie? But a gnome?" His deep brown eyes twinkle at mine, reminding me of the lights in the store, and of the Hanukkah song—"One for each night, they shed a sweet light."

Noah seems to shed a sweet light wherever he goes without even trying, but I'm okay in the dark, thank you very much. So I shake my head and try to get back on topic.

"My *question* is, what makes a gnome Jewish? Is it a new thing that I'm missing? Like Elf on the Shelf? Do all Texan Jews have a Gnome in the Home? Does he spy on you and report back to someone whether you've done your Hebrew homework? Or skipped synagogue?" My eyebrows knit together as I try to figure it out. It's a small thing, but I have to know.

Noah holds up a finger for me to wait a second as he goes to the window and takes Mordechai out, dusting him off a bit with the corner of his apron. "Look at his long white beard. Doesn't this scream rabbi to you? Can't you see him staying out late debating one line of Torah with his gnome rabbi friends? And then the rabbi's wife will get annoyed, but she married a Torah scholar on purpose, so she'll just take it out on her challah by kneading it extra hard. Somehow they make it work."

I shake my head and pick up a pickle, crunching down on it. "Clearly, you have an active imagination. I was just wondering, although now I want challah. And more pickles."

In my Jewish summer camp, they gave an award every week for the most ruach, or spirit. Noah seems like he's suffering from *too* much of it, and yet, I'm still stifling a smile, which I try hard to contain. I will *not* be charmed by him or his gnome, or this town, for that matter. But that doesn't mean I'm not going to eat. I have to give in to temptation sometimes, and right now the food is a safer temptation than Noah.

"Um, can I get some of that soup and maybe a knish, too?" I ask, making an impromptu decision and closing my menu.

He looks at me a little funny but nods. "Hope you're hungry," he says before dashing back into the kitchen. As he does, I take the opportunity to take a couple of selfies, pictures of the deli menu and decor, and text them to my friends and even my parents.

Yeah, I'm still super annoyed at them, but texting is easier than calling when I don't have much to say other than kvetching about how they made me come here while Josh gets to hang out with a cute girl and they get to check out restaurants or movies, or whatever they're doing in the city alone without me and Josh.

A second later, my dad texts back. *Put jalapeños and hot sauce in the matzah ball soup.*

I text back a green-faced emoji, indicating that the idea makes me sick to my stomach, but he responds right away. *Trust me.*

I'm rolling my eyes, but when Noah comes back with my soup and knish, I see what he means. They're huge. Each matzah ball is the size of a snowball and there are three of them. The knish is the size of my outstretched hand almost.

"Everything is bigger in Texas. It's cliché, but it's true," he says, giving me a huge spoon as well. "Anything worth doing is worth doing in Capital Letters. I did try to warn you. . . ." He shrugs and pulls out condiments from under the counter, including mustard and horseradish. "But far be it for me to discourage a paying customer. Just don't let my grandfather see you. He hates when people waste food, and I doubt you can put this all back. No offense."

I nod. "This is a weird question, but my dad said I should ask for jalapeños and hot sauce. Is he joking? Or is that a code word so I can get the secret menu? Like a speakeasy for Jewish food?"

Noah shakes his head. "We haven't changed the menu in decades. This is a traditional, old-school deli. No avocado toast here."

From the back, I can hear someone else coming through the swinging doors from the kitchen.

An older man wearing a yarmulke comes out and looks at me closely over his glasses. This must be Noah's grandfather. "Who did you say your dad was?"

"I didn't, but he's David Levin. He used to live here in Rosenblum when he was younger."

The man puts his towel down and laughs loudly. "Davey! Now a history professor in New York, right? Of course, right. He practically lived here during high school when his mother got the horses and didn't have as much time to cook, not that she was much of a cook anyways. Oy . . ."

"Zayde!" Noah admonishes his grandfather, his cheeks turning red. Good, at least I'm not the only one embarrassed tonight.

"It's true whether I say so or not. Just don't tell Sarah I said that. Okay? She's a nice lady. She does good work with those horses."

"She makes good pancakes," I say meekly.

"I'm sorry," Noah mumbles as his grandfather putters into the kitchen. "He thinks because he's old he can say whatever he wants."

"I *can* say whatever I want," his grandfather says from the other room.

"He's adorable," I say as his grandfather comes back with a jar of something and a dish of something else. "Jalapeños and hot sauce for the Yankee." He chuckles. "Be careful with those," he says as I hesitate. "I think your dad invented the combination on a dare."

"Did he lose the dare or win it?" I ask, putting a tiny bit of each in the soup, and yeah, it does add a nice kick, but I like most of my Jewish food bland as my Ashkenazi ancestors intended it. I can't imagine my boring dad being so daring either, but there's probably other things I don't know about him when he lived here, especially what went down between him and my grandmother—and why he left.

I'm still contemplating my dad's secret, daring hot-pepper-flavored history when I take a gulp of soup, which must have had too much hot sauce. "Ouch!" My mouth is burning and I'm waving my hand in front of my face. I gulp down water, but it doesn't help. If anything, it makes it worse, spreading the heat everywhere. Noah brings over a piece of challah.

"Definitely lost the dare."

"Eat this; it will help." Noah glances at his grandfather. "This is why we stick to the menu, Zayde," he says over his shoulder.

I nod and take a big bite of the soft, slightly sweet bread. He's right; it's much better than water. "I think I'll stick with the knish," I say, pouring some regular mustard on it and taking a bite, enjoying the soft potato filling with the slightly crusty exterior. "Mm. This is good!" I put a hand over my mouth so he doesn't see me chewing and talking at the same time.

He looks so proud of himself, I have to add after swallowing, "I mean for Texas."

At this point, the few older gentlemen in the deli are eavesdropping with interest. It's another thing that makes me feel like home. Next, they'll start complaining about their sciatica, or telling me about their grandchildren. All par for the course at synagogue, or the JCC where we belong.

But if Noah notices the eavesdroppers, nothing seems to dim his optimism, which is rather annoying. Until he looks around the mostly empty deli and his shoulders fall, a similar look to the other day when he was in the hot-dog costume with the platter of samples. "If only we had more customers. I'd say tell your friends, but that wouldn't do much good, would it, city girl? No one's coming to Rosenblum for soup. Jalapeños aren't going to solve that. This place is dead, and I'm not just talking about the elderly customers."

One of the older customers shoots him a disapproving look and tsks loudly.

"I didn't mean you, Mr. Saperstein!"

Mr. Saperstein grumbles loudly to his friends, but Noah ignores him and picks up my discarded bowl and takes it to the back, then starts cleaning the counters furiously. The other customers, all three of them, are standing up and saying goodbye to Noah's grandfather, who has come out of the kitchen to kibitz, or chat, with them.

I must glance over nervously because Noah just chuckles. "They're practically like uncles to me. Don't worry about it. They love to have something to complain about. They'll talk about me the whole way home, and they'll love it. I'm sure their grandchildren are much more successful and respectful. I think one is in med school already. I can't compete with that," he says with a pained look that disappears as soon as I spot it.

"Good luck with that hip replacement, Irv. Have a safe trip, Sol. I'll see you next week?" Noah's grandfather says.

"God willing, we'll see you next week, Abe," Sol says, hugging them all, as Noah walks around and pulls all the blinds down, then turns the sign on the door to Closed.

I put down money, not waiting for the check, and stand up to go, able to take a hint. "My grandmother is going to be picking me up soon. Thanks for everything. I'll see you around?"

"You can't go yet!" Noah's zayde, Abe, says, packing up something in a bag. "You loved the knishes, and you're going to need a taste of home at Sarah's. Lovely woman, can't cook, which is why your dad was so skinny . . ."

"You already said that, Zayde," Noah says, but rather than annoyed, his eyebrows are knitted together as if he is worried. He tries to get his grandfather to sit down, but the older man waves him off.

I'm about to say thank you again when Abe pulls a framed photo off the wall randomly. "Wait, wait," he says. "This, here, that's your dad when he worked here one summer."

"Wow, he never mentioned that," I say, poring over the photo. It's faded, but he's right, my dad is there, wearing a Nirvana shirt and an apron with the store's logo on it, and one of the flannel shirts I'd taken from him. He's got his arm around the other guys in the photo and is standing in front of what looks like a huge pile of potatoes.

"That's my dad," Noah says, pointing to the guy next to my dad. He's got a Houston Astros baseball hat on and a smile not unlike Noah's. They both look pretty proud.

There's a lightness about my dad I haven't seen in a while thanks to all the papers he's always grading and exams he's always writing, never mind the pressure to publish books and do research. This version of my dad is younger, yes, but more carefree and with more hair. It makes me wonder why he left this place that made him happy once upon a time, and what changed.

"We were on the news that year for creating the biggest latke in Texas, second biggest in the country. So much attention we got. You wouldn't want to eat it, though. It wasn't crisp enough, so not cooked all the way through. It was a waste of food, and I hate wasting food, but it drove a lot of customers here, and I donated some of the proceeds to the food bank, so it worked out. . . ."

"You should do that again," I say with a look around the empty deli, but Abe brushes me off.

"Do you know how long it took to peel so many potatoes? I was a lot younger then; we all were. Less arthritis, more energy."

He takes the photo and places it back on the wall where it was. "You tell your dad we were asking about him. He's a mensch, that one, or he would be, if he visited more. Tell him we've noticed."

Ouch. The Jewish guilt is strong with that one, so much so that Noah mouths "sorry" to me, but I shake my head. It's okay. I'm fluent in Jewish guilt, too, which is exactly how I ended up in Texas visiting my grandmother in the first place. All my parents had to do was remind me of the mitzvah of honoring the elderly a couple of times until I gave in and agreed to go, but that didn't mean I had to be happy about it.

Abe shuffles off back to the kitchen, leaving me and Noah alone. I feel as if I should offer to clean up or something, but that would be weird. I'm just a customer. And just visiting. And just not interested in forming any connections here. After all, I'm literally only here for a few days.

I take one more look around this special place with special people. It would be a shame if it didn't survive, but there's nothing really I can do in the few days that I'm here, so I say thank you one more time, grab my bag of goodies, and give an awkward wave to Noah before heading out. The door shuts behind me as my grandmother's car rolls up to take me away from the pickles, and any chance to spend more time with Noah or his gnome, which is probably for the best.

"Seriously?" I mumble. The alarm next to my bed is blasting Christmas music, and not the peaceful, quiet kind I can ignore. I didn't notice an alarm clock there, and I certainly didn't set it myself because I don't feel like rocking around *any* sort of tree, Christmas tree or not, until I've had some strong coffee. I fumble with the off button and wish I could keep it off the whole holiday season until I get home to New York.

For the first time, I wonder if the Grinch was just a marginalized Jewish kid forced to observe everybody else having a great time and rubbing it in his face. If so, *I get it,* not that I condone the Grinch's crime spree or anything, but I totally understand feeling left out during the holidays when you're surrounded by the Holly and the Jolly 24/7.

I myself am neither holly *nor* jolly, and a far cry from

merry, and I'm okay with that. It's not in my makeup. Luckily, Hanukkah is not about gumdrops either. It's a serious holiday about resistance, a religious miracle that led to the rededication of the temple, and staying true to your Jewish identity. That I can get behind.

After heading downstairs, I notice there's a whole lot more activity going on than yesterday. My grandmother is pacing, drinking her coffee and already dressed in work boots and a heavy coat, like she's been waiting for me.

"There's a bad frost; I could really use your help after breakfast," she says, worry lines evident on her forehead again. Sensing her distress, I eat a banana quickly, then run upstairs to put on my very own clothes, which apparently arrived on the doorstep when I was out last night with Noah. Well, not exactly with Noah, more like adjacent to Noah.

I help bring extra hay to the horses, fill their water bowls with warmer water, lay down blankets for them and on them, to make them more comfortable in a storm that my grandmother says is coming. While there is a chill in the air, the sky is bright and I'm not seeing any storm clouds, not that I'm questioning her.

After our chores, hot showers, and some more coffee, my grandmother turns on the local weather. The map is bright blue, but I don't know Texas geography, so I keep sipping the strong coffee until Nana grabs her keys and sighs. "Hannah, we better go into town and get a few supplies and groceries, just in case."

"Just in case what?" I ask. "I thought they said it would

just be a few inches. We don't even cancel school unless there's a foot of snow. Everything's open, and we go to Central Park for snowball fights and sledding. . . . It's pretty magical, actually. Nature, not store-bought seasonal joy . . ."

My grandmother walks briskly to her truck, and I follow. Once she's buckled in and backing up, she answers me. "The difference is, honey, that just one inch could put the town in a complete standstill. No one knows how to drive in it, and we don't have the right kind of tires or equipment to clear it either. When you're not used to things, it's harder to prepare and react."

She hums to herself along with the radio the rest of the way. Luckily, it's the Beatles channel on Sirius radio, and she's drumming her hands on the steering wheel as we go. While I don't know her that well, it seems like she's nervous and doesn't want to let on that she is, but as a New Yorker and a Jew, I reserve my right to worry preemptively, just in case I need to do so later. It saves me time and energy that I can put into more worrying.

We pull into a parking space about a block from the hardware store as someone else is pulling out. Other cars are circling like sharks looking for spaces. When we get out of the truck, there's a line out the door at the general store and a line at Blum's as well, although a smaller one. Other stores are closed already, like the antique store and the nail salon.

My grandmother gets in line and follows my gaze. "I need toilet paper, some salt for the driveway if they have any, and a few other things. Why don't you see if you can pick us up some challah and I'll make French toast and grilled cheese with it. . . . Feel free to get whatever else you want, too. Maybe some soup would be good on a cold night? If not, I have some cans at home."

She hands me a twenty-dollar bill, and I cross the street and stand in the back of the line. Yesterday the place was practically empty; today it's packed, leading me to wonder if every single person in town came out for supplies. After about ten minutes of just staring at the gnome in the window taunting me, I realize we have barely moved. I'm no closer to the gnome's pointy hat and his sparkly tunic than I was when I got here.

The people in front of me are starting to give up. "I got a text from my daughter that Kroger still has some bread. I think we should go," one of them says.

They exit the line as others are complaining to each other and debating leaving. I catch Noah's panicked eyes through the window. He's all alone behind the counter, although I can see some movement in the kitchen behind him, where someone is probably cooking or preparing the food.

He mouths "help" to me, and pushy New Yorker that I am, I worm my way to the front of the line and let myself in. "Excuse me, pardon me, sorry," I say to the people as I weave my way toward the door, elbows first.

When I do, he looks relieved. Little does he know, I'm not a great cook, or even a passable one, but at least I'm a warm body, which looks like what he needs to help get the line down.

He grabs an apron from behind the counter and hands it

to me. "Hannah! Please, please help. I'll give you all the pick-les you want if you'll help me out for a bit until things calm down. Please!"

I glance down at the gray apron, which has a dreidel on it and says *This Is How I Roll*.

"The pun will cost you extra pickles, and there's no way I'm wearing a hot-dog costume," I grumble, but I go over to greet the next customer, not waiting for instruction.

Noah shoots me a grateful glance and puts me in charge of fetching whatever it is the customers want, after I've washed my hands and discarded my coat. Soon we have a rhythm going.

"Six bagels: three everything bagels, one garlic, one rye, one plain," he shouts. "One potato knish, one spinach. Three latkes. One plain cream cheese."

I run around and put everything in a bag, and then he rings it up. We do this ten times, at least, dancing past each other behind the counter, as I sneak a glance here and there. Whenever I do, I catch him smiling at me like I may be the most delicious thing on the menu, which makes my face heat up like I've eaten the hot sauce all over again. Not good.

Do not react, do not blush, I tell myself, and try to focus on the task at hand. Be useful and then get out of there.

After his heated glance, I do my best to avoid eye contact and any and all sparks. How could I have sparks with some-one covered in cream cheese working his butt off? There's no point. This is it. He was desperate, so I stepped up to help, but it doesn't mean anything. I could never take someone seriously who is so into his commercialized version of Hanukkah, anyway, with the stupid gnome and puns, and his optimistic attitude and sunny smile in this wacky place. I mean, there's a reason most Jewish music is played in a minor key. We dwell in the dreary, revel in the bittersweet. Noah has no dark side, so I just can't relate. He's the Jewish form of jolly, like that ridiculous gnome.

There's a reason the sun and the moon don't hang out. They have very little to say to each other because they have completely different outlooks.

Finally, the line dissipates, and he walks over to the cooler and hands me a black cherry seltzer. "Thank you. I know it was weird to ask you to help, but I figured maybe it runs in the family. Your dad did work here after all. It was an impulsive move, but sometimes those are the best ones," he says, cracking his own drink open.

"I think the weirder thing is that I accepted," I admit, taking a big gulp of the bubbly drink. "I don't normally say yes to things I'm not good at. And I rarely say yes when I don't have a plan."

Noah drapes an arm on the now-empty counter. "How do you know you won't be good at something before you try it?"

I brush a curl off my forehead. "Experience? The fact that it's a risk? Or it's not in my skill set? Like my grandmother wants me to try riding a horse. I've literally fallen off the carousel in Bryant Park. It was awful. And it wasn't even a big carousel! Why would I want to try that with a real horse with a mind of its own? No way. Just being here in Texas is out of my comfort zone, and honestly, ask the horses. I'm a disaster! I don't need to throw dangerous sports and dangerous animals that weigh as much as a truck in the mix. I'm good, thanks. I'm a city mouse, happy to be going back to my apartment in a couple days. You can have your wide-open land and friendly neighbors. I'll be fine with the rats in the subway. They don't bother me and I don't bother them."

Noah's eyes grew wide. "You live in New York City. I'd say that's riskier than anything you will encounter in Rosenblum. Taxis probably go a whole lot faster than tractors. Also, rats are disgusting and carry disease."

I'm about to argue with him when I get a text from my grandmother. *Sorry, honey. I finished at the store and had to run home for the horses. A neighbor called and said Ringo got out. I'll swing back and get you later. It looked like you were busy and I didn't want to interrupt. It was very nice of you to help out Abe and his grandson.*

"I guess I'll take those pickles now," I say, making myself comfortable in a booth. "It may be a while."

Noah runs to the kitchen. I hear him chatting with his grandfather, who sounds tired, even through the doors. He comes back with a dish of promised pickles and an egg cream for each of us.

"I think we deserve this. What do you think?" His eyes are weary, but his tone is bright, even after all that work.

I hold up my drink and toast him. Of course the egg cream is delicious, but it seems even more special. "What's in this? I mean beyond the chocolate syrup, milk, and seltzer. I know what's in an egg cream, which has neither egg nor cream."

Noah's eyes dance with mischief. "A little nutmeg. To make it festive, like eggnog."

"You're really good at this," I say after taking a sip through a blue-and-white paper straw. "Did today help the bottom line? You had a ton of customers. They seemed happy once they finally got their food."

His shoulders sag. "It would take more than one freak snowstorm to save us, unfortunately. I mean, I'm glad to help provide the town with food and all that in an emergency; it's important work. Especially when the grocery stores run out of everything. I like to think of them having our matzah ball soup at home and feeling better. But it's not enough." He shakes his head.

I purse my lips, cold from the egg cream, unsure what to say. That's when it occurs to me that someone's missing, Noah's parents. "Noah, I noticed the sign says Blum and Sons, but it's actually just Blum and Grandson, right? Didn't your dad used to work here, with mine?"

Noah places his head on the back of the booth. "My dad is far too practical for this. He's an accountant, so *everything* is about the numbers. The numbers don't add up, Noah. We're in negative numbers. The numbers don't lie, Noah. Look at the cost-benefit analysis, the return on investment, and the graphs, charts, and spreadsheets, Noah," he says in a deep, disapproving voice, apparently in an impression of his dad. "He doesn't believe in me. The only one who does is my grandfather. My dad's always doubting me. I'm never good enough at anything."

"I'm sure that's not true," I say, although I can't be sure, not really. I don't know his family.

I make a sympathetic face, but he waves it off like it's not needed. "He was okay with me helping out my grandfather, but now that Zayde is older and getting tired, he wants us to sell the house and the deli and move to Houston so he can be closer to work. He wants me not to have any ties so I can go off to college somewhere far away and do something practical and boring, like him. He doesn't understand. Some things aren't about numbers at all."

I may not get what goes into running a deli, but generational arguments I get; in fact, I'm in the middle of one right now, it seems.

But all I say is "I hear Houston is cool. Lots of restaurants and museums. And lots of other Jews! So that's a bonus. It must be hard being the only Jews here."

Noah's normally cheerful lips turn downward as he brushes floppy hair out of his face. "But it's not home. The deli, Zayde, the general store . . . this town is home. It's been home for generations. Since the 1800s! I don't want to be the one who gives up. I can go to college nearby part-time and still manage the deli. Or not. I'll figure it out eventually."

I have an urge to hug him, which is so weird since I normally only hug kids under five when they scrape their knees, or my family. I open my mouth to find some other way of comforting him that doesn't involve touching him when my phone buzzes angrily, like a pack of annoyed bees.

"Just a sec," I say, holding up a finger for him to wait, assuming it's my grandmother again. But no, it's my mom.

"I've been trying to reach you!" she says all in one hurried breath. "Are you okay?"

"Why wouldn't I be?" I ask, playing with a napkin in front of me until it is shredded in a pile of white confetti, not unlike the flakes of snow now forming on the glass of the window and on the sidewalk. My mom, unlike my dad, has a flair for the dramatic; being a theater director will do that. The stakes are always high with my mom. My dad, on the other hand, is the calm one. Until he panics, I usually don't. I'm intense, but I'm pragmatic about reserving my energy for when it's truly warranted.

"Talk to your dad," she says, handing him the phone. And that's when I panic. No good conversation ever starts with *Talk to your dad*.

"What's going on?" I ask before he, too, asks if I'm okay. "Okay, someone needs to tell me what's up. I'm sitting in the deli eating pickles. There are signs everywhere about how to save someone from choking. I'm good, even if I choke on a pickle. Why wouldn't I be?"

My dad laughs a bit, but seemingly out of relief, not

humor. "There've been a ton of snow tornados and some freaky weather in Texas."

"Snow bomb cyclones!" my mom shouts into the phone in case *snow tornadoes* wasn't scary enough.

"Yes, that's what I meant," my dad says. "We've lost touch with your grandmother."

"Yeah, the service at the ranch is awful. I'm sure she's fine, right?"

"Probably," my dad says, but he sounds worried. "I think you should stay where you are until we can reach her."

My dad's loud enough that Noah can probably hear, but I repeat it anyway. "Yes, Dad. I can stay here at the deli for a bit, where apparently you worked. Not that you ever mentioned it."

"I tell you about my deli days every time we get pastrami and they cut it wrong," he jokes.

"Oh, I guess I wasn't listening," I say. "Anyway, I assume they won't mind if I stay here."

"Good. Please thank Abe for me."

My dad and mom take turns telling me they love me before hanging up and trying my grandmother again. Now I'm really worried. Like officially, seriously worried. I clearly didn't worry enough earlier, which was my first mistake.

As if sensing my unease, Noah puts the closed sign on the door and heads back to the kitchen. He returns with two big mugs of something. "Chicken noodle soup. We're out of matzah balls. They went fast today."

"It seems we're getting in a habit of you plying me with

carbs when things suck. You'll be out of soup pretty soon. I tend to have bad luck these days."

He grins, then pulls out the spoons from his apron. "That's what I do best. Oh! I almost forgot the most awesome part."

He scurries to the kitchen, which is now quiet. When he comes back, it's with a plate of latkes with applesauce and sour cream.

"I didn't know which you prefer," he admits. "People are usually strongly in one camp or another."

My eyes tear up, partially because they smell delicious and look wonderful, and partially because my mom and I usually make a huge batch of latkes every year and it's kind of our thing, but Noah doesn't need to hear that, so I manage a small smile that feels more like a grimace and spear a latke, putting it on my plate.

"The answer is, of course, Team Sour Cream for life," I tell him, taking a big dollop and putting it right on top. "Sour cream brings out the best in them. It's not dessert."

Unsurprisingly, Noah grabs the container of applesauce for himself. "I like them sweet," he says.

"And that's everything you need to know about our differences, country mouse."

"Country mouse?" he says between bites.

"Yeah, it was a kids' book about a city mouse and a country mouse that went to visit each other. I used to like it when I was little, but I never understood why *anyone* would give up living in the city."

"And now?" he asks. "Did you change your mind?"

I shake my head after taking another delicious bite of the latke coated with sour cream, the tang of it a sharp reminder. "Rosenblum has its charms, I'll give you that, for a short visit."

Noah puts a hand on his chest like I've wounded him, but he grins widely. "As one of Rosenblum's official charms, I'll take that as a compliment. And insist you try our homemade applesauce, because it makes the sour cream that much better."

I'm about to banter some more, to take my mind off my grandmother, when my phone dings again and it's her. "Nana! Are you okay?"

"Yes, yes, I'm fine. I didn't have my phone with me when I was taking care of the horses. I plugged it in to charge and ran out to the barn."

"How are Paul and Ringo?" I ask, realizing that I do actually care about the huge, manure-producing animals, despite what my brother thinks.

"They're spooked about the storm. I think that's why Ringo ran away, but they will be fine. I put them in the barn for the night with blankets and everything else they need."

"Good," I say, playing with the sour cream left on my plate and pushing the applesauce to the side. Noah raises an eyebrow and I flash him a thumbs-up, so he takes our plates away without another word about my choice in condiments.

Nana hesitates. "Listen, honey, I don't know if you've talked to your parents, but the storm's gotten worse. They're expecting huge amounts in the northeast. Your flight Sunday has been canceled. In fact, thousands of flights have been canceled all over the country. It's a mess."

"What?" I say, horrified at this news. "I was supposed to be home in time for Hanukkah! I had plans with my friends and my parents. We have traditions, stuff we look forward to all year!"

Noah comes out of the kitchen and looks at me with something that seems like pity at first and then interest, or intrigue. It's hard to tell.

My grandmother speaks softly. "I'm sorry you're disappointed, but I hope you'll look on the bright side. We'll have a nice long visit here. I've spoken to Abe, and you may have to stay there tonight because the roads are still icy and he doesn't think it's a good idea for me to drive right now."

"In the deli?" I ask, looking around at the vinyl booths and hard floors. I'm not a great sleeper anyway, so I don't see how I can manage. Not that I want my grandmother to drive in dangerous conditions.

"No, sweetie, they have the whole building. There's an apartment above the deli. You can sleep on the couch."

"You don't think that's weird?" I whisper into the phone. "I barely know them."

My grandmother laughs. "We've known the Blum family forever. They're not strangers. We take care of each other in a small town. Just sit tight and you'll be fine."

I grumble my thanks, but my heart has fallen. There go my plans for Hanukkah, for seeing my camp friends, hanging out in the city with Abby and Becky, and all the baking and cooking I like to do with my mom and dad. It may not be gourmet or professional, or even edible sometimes, but it's our thing. Never mind lighting the candles and everything else. Hanukkah is officially ruined.

"Snow in Texas? See! That's what I mean about my luck," I say, putting my head in my hands as Noah sits across from me in the booth.

"I'll make you a deal," he says finally.

His voice is so determined, I can't help it. I look up into his eyes. "What kind of deal?"

"It looks like you're going to be spending Hanukkah here, or at least part of it."

I wince at the truth of his words, but I make a gesture to him to continue with his proposal. "Yeah, I guess so. What are you suggesting?"

Here's where Noah gives me the full force of his applesauce-fueled smile. It's a smile so devious and innocent at the same time that I can't help but be drawn in, so I lean closer. "What do you have in mind?"

As this is someone who has willingly put himself in a hot-dog costume without complaint, I expect he has very few boundaries, but I have plenty to spare.

"I have to tell you that I can't do anything that will affect my chances of getting into college. Nothing illegal, unethical, immoral, or offensive."

"Okay . . . ," he says. "That's not what I'm proposing at all. Let me show you the magic of Hanukkah, right here in Rosenblum. There's no way you—I mean *we* can't celebrate it right here. It may even be your best Hanukkah ever! Courtesy of Mordechai, my gnome, and me."

I roll my eyes. "I doubt it. In fact, I'd probably rather sulk in peace. No offense, but your idea of magical is probably not the same as mine."

"You don't know that," he counters. "Just like you don't know if you can ride a horse. Come on, what else are you going to do here?"

I cross my arms over my chest and take a deep breath. "I guess I don't have any other plans now, so I will consider your offer. But what's my part of the bargain? What do you get in return for the merriment?"

Noah beams at me. "One, I get to be right, which I enjoy very much. I'd honestly do it for the bragging rights alone, because you're going to have an amazing time. And two, well, I hate to ask for help, but I think Zayde needs a break."

"You don't have any other help?" I ask.

"Well," Noah answers, "we usually have an awesome couple who works with us, especially on Shabbat so my grandfather can observe it. But José and Consuela went to Mexico to spend Christmas with their family. They're not back until after the New Year. Interesting fact: When Consuela's mom was dying, she told her that they were secretly Jewish, that their ancestors fled Spain during the Inquisition. They lit candles and didn't eat pork or shellfish. She never thought about it, but it made total sense once she knew. There are a bunch of crypto Jews in the Southwest."

"Interesting," I agree, but don't commit to anything yet.

Noah sinks down a bit in his seat and sighs. "The truth is that I'm worried about my grandfather, and I could really use help for as long as you're here. I think we make a good team. And to be absolutely honest, we can't afford to close the deli, even for a week. We normally make most of our money this time of year, when the town is lit up for the holidays and the weekend visitors come. So this is me begging."

He flashes me puppy-dog eyes that shouldn't work. And yet, they kinda do, despite my best efforts to resist his official Rosenblum charm. Still, I fold my arms over my chest, pretending to be unimpressed. But it's no good. I can't say no when so much is at stake for him and when it's in my power to do such a huge mitzvah.

I hold out my hand. "You don't need to beg. I'll do it. You have a deal. *Only* because your grandfather is adorable and I'd like to help you save the deli. Also, I have nothing better to do in Rosenblum. But don't think that you'll be successful in getting me to enjoy Hanukkah here. It would take more than a miracle for that to happen. . . ."

6

Noah's matzah balls may be pillowy, but his sleeper
sofa sure isn't, which I notice as soon as I see it from the hall.
The springs are practically visible. He puts his head down,
like he's embarrassed, as he leads me up the back stairs to the
apartment he sometimes shares with his grandfather if he's
working late at the deli.

"My parents live in a newer house on the other side of
town, so I'm going to crash here, too. Normally, I'd take the
sofa bed, but since you're the guest, I'll sleep in the office," he
says, taking off his jacket, then holding out his hand for mine
to hang in the closet.

As he faces the closet, I glance around, and wow. There
are dreidels of multiple materials and sizes, several menorahs,
some old and simple-looking, some with dinosaurs, dogs, and
bears. I even spy a Sasquatch menorah. Is Bigfoot even Jewish?

Oy. I can't believe I am even wondering that. It's the power of Noah's ability to turn everything on its head.

Blue and white tinsel hangs all over the mantel and in between doorways. Moreover, there are gnomes. Lots of gnomes. Apparently, Mordechai has a lot of siblings and a large extended family who decided to come over and not leave until the end of the holiday.

"What do you think?" he asks, eyes wide with anticipation as he spreads open his arms and turns around slowly, taking it all in. "Oh, wait! I haven't shown you the best part!" He practically trips on the way to the light switch, shutting them all off, then putting on some sort of machine that shoots projections of Hanukkah imagery in laser form onto the ceiling. Dreidels, stars, and menorahs take form and bounce around above us.

"That's the best part?" I choke out. "I take it you did all this? Or someone came in and threw up Hanukkah spirit all over the apartment."

He chuckles. "Yeah, I started collecting this stuff a couple years ago, to help cheer up the deli and my grandfather. He misses his friends, especially around holidays. You know, there used to be a nice-sized Jewish community in Rosenblum."

"Well, that's sweet, if a little misguided," I say, which is pretty much the most polite thing I can manage. It's literally the opposite of how I like my holiday, which is quiet, dignified, and meaningful.

I glance at the couch, which is covered in a blanket with the Star of David and a couple of Hanukkah-themed pillows.

I move a pillow and sit down, directly on a Hanukkah robot. "Ouch!"

"Oh, let me get that, sorry," he says as the robot starts to sing "The Dreidel Song" before he shuts it down.

I clear my throat. "I didn't know that about Rosenblum. Although, I guess it makes sense. Since your family helped found it, there must have been other Jews who settled here originally," I say as I'm thinking aloud. "What happened?"

"Well, apparently, people moved away for jobs or to be closer to family, the oldest generation died, and then they went from having a synagogue with a full-time rabbi to a part-time rabbi, then just to an occasional rabbinical student. Then the rabbinical student stopped coming when she wasn't needed anymore. And then they closed the synagogue altogether. The general store used to be owned by a Jewish family as well. They came here as merchants in the 1860s, but well, they sold it when my grandfather was a kid. Our deli started off as a meat market way back when, but we eventually turned it into a deli in the 1920s rather than sell it."

"That's sad," I say. "If that happened in New York, you could just go to another temple. We've got plenty of them."

"Yeah, not so much here. The closest one is about forty miles from here, and the older people don't necessarily drive as much, especially at night, so it's a real challenge. I had to do most of my bar mitzvah lessons online . . . because it was too difficult to get to the Hebrew tutor every week. Anyway, the community eventually decided to sell the building. It's now a church, which is nice, I guess, because at least it's being used for worship and the building is being maintained, rather than torn down and turned into a laundromat or a parking lot. A nearby temple was even completely moved to Austin by truck in multiple parts so a new community could use it."

"So the older gentlemen who come into the deli? They used to live here?" I think back to their warm embraces and how at home they looked in their booth, like they had been going there for years.

"Yes, they went to school with my grandfather. Now they try to come by a couple times a month to see him and to come to the deli, but it's not enough to sustain us, or sustain him, not since my bubbe died. So"—he gestures to the decorations—"it's the least I can do."

I snort, which is, I admit, not the most attractive sound. "Commercialized Hanukkah? Buying out the entire Hanukkah section of Target? He doesn't think it's a little ridiculous?"

Noah sticks his lip out a little, like I've hurt his feelings. "Just because something's ridiculous doesn't mean it's not appreciated. I'd rather he laugh than cry. He misses my grandmother a lot. She made Hanukkah special for him, so now I try to do that in my own way."

I shrug and hug a Hanukkah pillow to me, before putting it on the other side of the couch and giving it a plumping. "Well, I hope it works for him, but I don't think it will do much for me . . . but don't worry, I'll still help you out at the deli. I promised."

Noah's face turns serious for a moment as he sits down

next to me on the sofa. "It's more than that. Since the temple closed, our deli is the last remnant of Jewish life in this town. If it disappears, so do we. So now you see why it's so important to keep it open."

I'm about to say something when the door from the bedroom opens and Zayde Abe wanders into the room in his slippers and a fluffy robe. "What do you think of the decorations? Isn't my grandson a little *meshuggeneh*?" He chuckles and messes up Noah's hair affectionately.

I hold out my pointer and thumb about three inches apart from each other. "Maybe a little? It is a whole lot of Hanukkah in here. It's not like it's even one of the major holidays. What do you do for Passover? Bring in live frogs? Flood the living room with red seawater?"

Zayde laughs and turns on the kettle. "I'm going to make some tea. You want?"

Noah and I both decline as his grandfather makes his tea, then heads back to his bedroom wishing us good night.

"I'll make you a Hanukkah fanatic, just like me," Noah says before going into the bathroom with a toothbrush.

When he's gone, I take the opportunity to look around the apartment some more. When I look beyond the cheesy decorations, I see a lot of family photos. Noah, even skinnier and shorter with a Torah and a tallis at what must be his bar mitzvah.

A much younger-looking Zayde with a bride and groom dancing the hora at a wedding, who I'm assuming are Noah's parents. Other photos show an old-fashioned black-and-white photo of the deli from a long time ago, maybe the 1920s. True to Noah's word, this photo shows a bustling place full of customers of all ages noshing and kibitzing. It's clear it was an important part of the Jewish cultural life at the time. Through the window in the photo, you can even see Yiddish posters on the movie theater across the street if you squint, as well as the general store, then called Saltzstein Mercantile Store.

The final photo on the mantel is of another bride and groom under a chuppah in what looks like the 1960s. That must be Zayde and Noah's bubbe, beaming at each other as they take part in the ceremony that joined their lives together.

To me, these family milestones signify much more about Jewish life than a gnome or some blue garland, but maybe it's like the sour-cream-and-applesauce debate. To each their own. Or maybe Noah is trying to fill in Jewish life where it's now on the brink of disappearing.

I vow to myself to be nonjudgmental. Jewish culture, life, and people are all around me in New York, infused in my day-to-day. I've never even thought that much about it; it's just the background music, the soundtrack to my life. It's there when I need it, running through my veins, something I can take for granted.

Noah has to make his own music. He's practically a one-man band.

I nod, committed to not being judgy, no matter how completely cringe he is being. My incredibly strong resolve lasts exactly one whole minute. That is, until the door to the bathroom opens and out walks Noah in obnoxious, bright blue Hanukkah pajamas with menorahs all over them and, worse, a flap on his bottom that says *Happy Hanukkah.* Not that I am trying to look at his butt, but really, who can help it if you put words on it and a menorah!

He has literally made his butt a billboard for the holiday.

My eyes must be bugging out of my head, until I shield them and try not to blush, because he laughs loudly, then jumps onto the sofa, grabbing the remote control and going to the DVR cue to check out what he's recorded. At least that's what I assume he's doing when I once again open my eyes.

"Seriously?" I ask. "Do you think those pajamas are what Judah Maccabee envisioned we'd be honoring his legacy with? A great miracle certainly Did Not Happen when they made those!" Rather than look contrite at all, he's still laughing.

"How do you feel about the Rugrats Hanukkah special? Oh, or there's a Hallmark Hanukkah movie I haven't seen yet."

"That's it! I don't want anyone else to wish me a happy Hanukkah until tomorrow, when it's actually Hanukkah! This means Rugrats, Gnomes, Hallmark, or your behind. Especially that one . . ."

I throw a Hanukkah pillow at him and head to the bathroom with my own toothbrush, shutting the door on him, his over-the-top holiday spirit, and his cute butt, not that I would ever admit that I thought that. Especially now.

Either it's my imagination or he's still laughing at me

through the door, but when I exit the bathroom, the sofa bed is set up. On the bed is a note. Trust Noah to be so dramatic that a text or a simple conversation isn't enough.

Remember, tomorrow is Night One of Hanukkah. That means I have 8 nights to change your mind.

And I have eight nights to remain right, I think as I doze off on the bed, tired enough not to bother to turn off the Shalom Sesame Street Hanukkah episode playing on the TV.

Night One of Hanukkah

I wake up to a jelly doughnut on the counter with a note from Noah. *In this house we pregame!* His handwriting is bold and excited, rather like him. Exclamation points and smiley faces everywhere. On the other side of the doughnut is a key, presumably to the deli, and a stick figure drawing of me in an apron that says *Employee of the Month*.

I stick the key in my bag and bite into the doughnut, catching the escaping jelly with my hand. I'm not arguing with the idea of pregaming, even though I had just told him I didn't want to celebrate Hanukkah yet. It turns out jelly doughnuts, or sufganiyot, as they are called in Israel, are pretty darn persuasive, no matter what you call them.

My mom always gets fresh ones from either the Doughnut

Plant on the Lower East Side or some other gourmet place she reads about, but inevitably, my dad will come home with some from his favorite coffee cart guy, too, until we have more than we can eat.

I take another bite. The doughnut tastes different here in Texas, and I don't think it's just the way the Texas water affects the yeast; it's how being away from home is affecting me. Everything is different.

Noah also left an extra menorah and candles for me to take home, probably assuming correctly I forgot to bring one of my own. I run my fingers over the wood block painted blue and the bright yellow clay candleholders that still have the fingerprints of a child imprinted on them. I then turn it over and see his name and a date. Yup. It looks like he made it himself when he was in kindergarten, if my math is correct. My mom has one of mine just like it, covered in wax from years of use. I imagine a much smaller Noah making it for his parents and presenting it to them proudly and a weird feeling washes over me, one I can't identify. It's somewhere between fondness and, ugh, something more. It's the something more I'm not willing to recognize—not here in this small town and not with Noah of all people.

I may have slept until seven a.m., but apparently, Noah is already showered and in the deli, according to the back of the note. Of course, Noah's a morning person. He probably wakes up singing and smiling. Just another one of our differences.

I also have a text from my grandmother saying the roads

are finally clear and that she'll be picking me up soon after my shift downstairs.

I'll admit, I'm nervous and pretty curious as to what Noah will pull off on such short notice. When I head downstairs to the deli, my apron is already waiting for me, hanging up on a peg behind the counter.

"Good morning, Miss Hannah," Gillian from the antique shop says from her place on line. Everyone seems to call each other miss or mister here, but it seems more affectionate than formal.

"How'd your grandmother fare during the storm? Any trees down?" Nancy from the hardware store asks from the counter.

"She's fine, thank you, ma'am." I remember this time to address her as such. "One of the horses got out, but he's back home now," I say while washing my hands at the sink, then head to the register to relieve Noah. Three days here and I'm already on a first-name basis with more people than in several years after moving to our new apartment in New York. I'm not sure how I feel about it, so I look down and try to concentrate on my task at hand, which is the morning rush. Unfortunately, it's not too much of a rush, just a few people wanting coffee and local shopkeepers and employees coming in for a bagel or pastry. Most everyone is in a rush—well, the Texas version, which means they engage in ten minutes of chitchat as opposed to thirty minutes. But it's clear that they are fond of Abe, Noah, and now, for some reason, that has even extended to include me.

About an hour later, things have slowed down enough that Noah has poured a couple of coffees for us and set them at a booth. Of course, he puts a ton of milk and sugar in his. I raise an eyebrow, but he sips it as I take mine black. No frills, just the strong taste of the fresh beans.

"I don't know how you can drink it black. Between this and sour cream, and your ridiculous stance on savory kugel, I am ready to say that you definitely need some sweetness in your life. Starting with tonight."

"Should I be nervous?" I ask. "Is there a witch with a candy house somewhere?"

"No hints." He wags his finger at me. "Just remember they're more afraid of you than you are of them."

"Who are? Bees? Sharks? Alligators? I read there are alligators in Texas. Oh, and snakes! What do they have to do with Hanukkah? For the record, I'm allergic to llamas, horses, and tinsel. They all make me break out in hives. For different reasons, obviously."

Noah tilts his head as if trying to understand. "Why in the world would I be introducing you to llamas? And no one is allergic to tinsel."

"Tinsel makes me sneeze and itch. Too much holiday cheer and synthetic material."

"And what about your fixation with llamas?" he asks. "Do you even have llamas in New York?"

"I met one once on a school field trip to the Bronx Zoo." I shudder. "It Did Not Go Well. But I didn't know there was such a thing as a Hanukkah robot, so I had to let you know, just in case. Who knows what you're planning."

He gives me a slow grin. "I'm usually more spontaneous than into planning, but all will be revealed, Hannah. Just remember, keep an open mind and leave everything up to your Hanukkah elf."

"That's where you've lost me again. There are no Hanukkah elves. Or Jewish elves, for that matter . . . The Maccabees were resistance fighters who had to stand up for their religious freedoms. There was a temple that needed to be rededicated and the miracle of the oil lasting for eight days. That's the story of Hanukkah. No elves involved."

"What about Frodo and Merry and Pippin? They constantly complain about how they're lost and eat two breakfasts. That sounds pretty Jewish to me. . . ."

"*The Lord of the Rings* is not a Jewish text, and even if it were, hobbits are not elves. Goodbye, Noah. Oh, and thank you for lending me your menorah. I promise I'll take care of it." I hang up my apron and wave as my grandmother pulls her truck up slowly to the sidewalk. There's no ice left on the street, but based on the way her eyes are squinting in concentration, she's not taking any chances.

I get into the car, and to my surprise, there's a big, furry black-and-white dog in the back seat. He wags his tail and then lies down in a ball with a sigh.

"Friend of yours?" I ask.

My grandmother laughs. "He wandered up last night,

cold and hungry in the middle of the storm. I called the local animal shelter. I'm hoping to find his owners, but if not, I guess he can stay. He's very friendly, and it's been a while since I've had a dog. Maybe it's what your grandfather called bashert, fated to be."

As if he understands, the dog sits up straight and puffs out his chest.

"Just like you staying for an extra-long visit. Maybe that's bashert, too. I've never had you here by yourself, and never had you here for such a long visit. I'm sure once you start college next year it will be too difficult for you to get away."

I don't answer, but the dog thumps his tail in approval.

"Aren't you a good boy, Elvis!" she says.

"Elvis?" I ask. "You're fated to have a dog soulmate called Elvis?"

"I'm branching out because I ran out of Beatles." She laughs, and the dog howls along. "Here, give him some cheese." She hands me a piece. "He likes it."

"I hate to agree, Nana, but I think you belong to him now, and vice versa, although I think it has more to do with treats and less to do with fate," I say as the dog very gently takes the cheese out of my hand and gives it a lick for good measure.

"Well, as the human Elvis would say, I can't help falling in love." My grandmother, now smiling and looking more confident behind the wheel, pulls into her long driveway and lets the dog out. Rather than run away, he trots after her toward the barn. "Um, how does he feel about horses?" I ask.

The dog runs right toward them and barks until Ringo and Paul back away toward their respective stalls. "Whoa." He's much smaller but doesn't seem to know that, or care. He's asserted himself as boss.

"I think he must have some shepherd or collie in him," my grandmother says. "It could come in handy."

"Most of the dogs in my neighborhood are small, yappy ones, so I wouldn't know," I say, "but he does look more useful than they are. . . ."

That's when Elvis decides to be less useful and go to sleep in the tack room on a stack of blankets. I guess his skills begin and end at bossing around other animals, kind of like mine. Only, Elvis seems more successful with horses than I am with people.

My grandmother doesn't seem to mind, as she's already hauling hay or whatever it's called that she's doing to it. Not unlike Noah's grandfather, my grandmother is also stubborn and unwilling to slow down, despite the fact that I catch her holding her back at one point. She's in more pain than she lets on. I'm not surprised. Taking care of horses is no joke. The piles of hay, saddles, and bags of feed are really heavy.

Without being asked this time, I pitch in, fetching water but start to worry what will happen when I'm not around, and just like that, I have another person and dog I'm connected to, despite my best efforts to remain unattached, and it's only been a few days. The sooner I can get out of Rosenblum and back to my regular, real life with fewer farm animals and more subways, the better. But that doesn't mean that I won't talk to my dad about getting her some help around the ranch. Maybe she'd finally listen to him.

The rest of the day goes by in a blur of chores, trying to refresh my email, and texting with Abby and Becky, until I look at the clock in the barn and realize that I only have an hour to get ready for whatever it is Noah has planned. Do I wear jeans or leggings, or something nicer? I don't think I even brought anything nicer. It's impossible to know where he's taking me or what we're going to do, which is probably exactly the point. Little does he know that I'm not great with surprises. I'm also not great with people being late. It's a control-freak thing. I can tell just from spending time with Noah that he probably doesn't have the same issue. He's all spur of the moment. Who else would meet a strange girl, hire her, and dedicate eight days to showing her the "joys" of Hanukkah?

It reminds me of a theory my dad read about how everyone is either a "Chaos Muppet" or an "Order Muppet." Noah is absolutely a Muppet of Chaos, an Ernie or Grover, while I crave order, organization, and even like pigeons, not unlike Ernie's roommate, Bert. File that under reason three hundred why this won't work out. While Noah may be fun for a few days of distraction, I refuse to give in to the chaos for longer than that.

At 5:00 p.m., I call my parents right on time. "I can see you, but I can't hear you," my mom says, looking over her purple-rimmed glasses at me.

"I like your glasses!" I say, but she just shakes her head like she still can't hear me.

Then my dad grabs the phone and fiddles with a few things. I can see his eyes crinkle in amusement when he hands the phone back to my mom. "She had the volume turned down."

We all laugh until Josh beeps in, and I accept him to our three-way FaceTime call. Josh is still in his dorm room with his baseball-themed menorah, my parents have our artistic one that my mom bought at the Jewish Museum, and I have Noah's little-kid one.

All three have candles in them and are ready to be lit. "One, two, three," my mom counts down, ever the theater director. "Baruch atah Adonai," we all begin to sing.

It's not the same, but at least I can hear their voices chanting the Hanukkah blessings along with me, my dad's slightly off key, my mom's loud and melodic musical-theater belt, and Josh's easy baritone.

"Okay, Josh, you can open one of your presents," my mom says with an apologetic look at me. "I'm so sorry, honey. I'd sent Josh's gifts in advance to school, but I thought you'd be here to open them in person. Oh, I did send you a Starbucks gift card via email!"

"Go ahead, Josh," I say to my brother, who also shoots me a look of pity before tearing into the blue-and-silver wrapping paper and discovering a new set of wireless headphones. "Thanks, Mom and Dad." He holds up the box. "These will be great, especially when Ari snores," he says, joking about his roommate, who is back in California. Then everyone goes quiet again.

"It's okay, Mom," I reassure her, without bothering to remind her that the nearest Starbucks is thirty long miles away. "It was never about the presents. Okay, maybe it was when I was little . . . but I just miss being there with you guys, and my friends. There's this new pop-up restaurant on the Lower East Side with Hanukkah-themed menus and mocktails. It's stuff like that I miss, too."

My mom gets a little teary until my dad takes over the conversation and changes the subject to something our cranky neighbor upstairs said on the elevator about us setting off the fire alarm every year with burning latkes and that Trader Joe's sells perfectly good ones we can put in the oven or an air fryer, no oil needed. Soon, we're all laughing and the time has gone by way too fast, and my grandmother pokes her head into my room to remind me it's almost time to meet Noah.

And, of course, at 7:00 p.m., about fifteen minutes later than planned, Noah rolls up in a blue pickup. On the back of the truck is a bumper sticker that says *Blum and Sons, Putting the Deli in Delicious since 1921* and another one saying *Shalom Y'All Means Y'All* with a rainbow Pride flag. But the most surprising thing is the obvious one.

"You can drive?" I ask as he opens the door and his long legs stretch out.

He knits his eyebrows together. "Um, yeah. How do you think I go back and forth between the deli and my house and school?"

"Public transportation? A school bus? I assumed you have

a bus system or a horse and trolley or whatever. I didn't think you drove. None of my friends drive yet. Oh, other than Becky, but that's because she was babysitting on Long Island during the summer and had to learn."

Noah rolls his eyes. My signature gesture must be contagious. "Nope. Oh, city mouse, you have a lot to learn about country life. Folks here learn how to drive tractors at fourteen. Cars and trucks are way easier. But that's for another lesson. Right now, we have an important performance to attend. We don't want to miss the curtain. The singers get cranky if they don't get snacks on time."

"Llamas get cranky?"

"There are no llamas, Hannah," he says, walking over to the passenger side of the truck and opening the door for me. "There were never any llamas involved in this night's performance."

I guess this part of Texas etiquette I could get used to. Uber drivers don't usually open doors for customers.

Once in the cab, I buckle up, and it's a very good thing that I do. Noah starts the truck and drives like he does everything, impulsively. He's fast, hugging each curve in the very windy road, stopping quickly for a cow to cross the road, then speeding up again until an armadillo crawls across, at which time he slams on his breaks.

"Whoa. Noah, seriously. Where did you learn to drive? A video game?"

"Sorry." He glances over at me and sees my grimace.

"There isn't much traffic around here, and I know the roads pretty well. . . ."

"Please watch the road. I'll just be here reciting the Traveler's Prayer to myself . . . just to be sure we actually arrive wherever it is we're actually going. Y'hi ratzon milfanecha . . . May it be your will . . . ," I start, but stop as I don't remember the whole thing. However, I think I make my point because he slows down.

"Sorry. I get excited when I'm going somewhere fun, but I'll slow down for the New Yorker. Although I thought city folks were always in a rush."

Despite his promise, we go flying over a big bump in the road, sending us airborne.

"Ouch!" I say, hitting my head on the roof of the cab. "There are no armadillos in the city, and we don't stop for rats."

He winces but leans over to turn music on. I brace myself for holiday music, but instead, it's normal music from his phone, although a little loud. "Anything special you want to hear?" he asks.

"Something morose?"

"Got it, the musical embodiment of sour cream," he says, putting on some Olivia Rodrigo, which perfectly hits the spot, balancing out whatever overly sweet Hanukkah thing he has planned. All her songs about love lost and pain remind me of another reason I can't get attached to anyone here. It would hurt too much to leave.

We listen in silence for two songs until he pulls into the

parking lot of an elementary school and jumps out. I go to open my own door, but he walks around the truck so quickly, he beats me to it.

"Follow me," he says, his long legs a few steps ahead of mine. He's practically bouncing again, Tigger-like in his excitement, reaching the front door of the school and then opening it, gesturing for me to follow him inside.

"Okay, this is weird," I comment as my feet make a ton of noise on the linoleum in the empty hallways of the school. "Entering an empty school is a good way to die in a horror movie."

We stop in front of the auditorium. Even from the outside, I hear the high-pitched sounds of small children chattering. Kids, not llamas, so that's a point in his favor.

His smile is contagious as he pauses before opening the door. "I admit that I had a little help with this one. Your grandmother told my grandfather that you really like kids and want to be a teacher. I also admit, I was surprised."

"Why? Kids are awesome. They have no pretense about them. They say what they mean. If they think your outfit is ugly, they'll say it. And they want to learn. They get excited about everything. By the way, that's totally cheating by asking my grandmother."

"No it's not! I'm using the information that's available to me," he says with an innocent pout.

I push my hair out of my face and shrug. "Fine. I do want to be an elementary school teacher, but I have to get an undergrad degree first, so it will probably be a while. My dad's a professor, but I prefer little kids."

"That's cool," Noah says. "I guess I didn't think you'd like kids because of their capacity for holiday cheer, but I stand corrected." He opens the door with a huge smile. Inside the auditorium are about twenty kids, maybe kindergarteners or first graders, all in red, green, and white. In the audience are parents, grandparents, and squirmy siblings of all ages. The kids on the stage are absolutely adorable in their white tights, headbands, and bow ties, but I have no idea what they have to do with Noah's promise to help me celebrate Hanukkah. It looks like I've just wandered into the middle of a school Christmas concert.

Noah finds us a pair of seats in the back since the performance is underway. We duck down and quietly sit as the kids start singing "Frosty the Snowman" followed by "Rudolph the Red-Nosed Reindeer." I smile and clap all the way through multiple verses.

Just as I'm about to whisper to Noah to ask why we're here, the teacher, a wavy-haired blond woman in her twenties in a red top and black pants and reindeer ears, comes to the front of the stage, and Noah gestures that we should head there as well. "Just give us one minute!

"Thank you, Kimberly—I mean, Miss Atkinson," he says, handing over a shopping bag to her. I try to peek inside it but can't see anything. The kids scramble to the wings of the auditorium, and I hear a lot of activity and giggling coming from the sides.

"What is this?" I ask, sitting in a front-row seat with a reserved sign on it, but he just points toward the stage, where the kids are lining up again. This time they are each hugging a blank piece of paper to their chest and looking very serious as they walk with their backs straight, one behind the other.

Kimberly walks to the center of the stage and smiles out at us. "The first graders of Rosenblum Elementary are delighted to close the concert by presenting a special song for you this Hanukkah."

She sits down at the piano and holds out her hand to count to three. "One, two. three."

Right on cue, the kids start yelling or singing loudly, somewhat off-key "I have a little dreidel, I made it out of clay, when it's dry and ready, oh Dreidel I will PLAY" and so on, and so on, and so on until the kids are clapping, their faces red from the efforts of singing. The song seems like it will never end, but I'm weirdly okay with that. This is the joy I've been missing.

Noah claps along and mouths the words with them until the very end, when Kimberly gestures for them to hold up their papers. One by one they turn them around to read *Happy Hanukkah Han!*

I clap loudly for them, not for Noah. "Very cute, but manipulative. Kids and puppies are the oldest trick in the book," I say under my breath to him. "And where's the rest of my name? How do I even know this was designed for me? Maybe they were supposed to be singing for Han Solo."

"Ouch! Tough audience," he says. "First of all, Harrison

Ford has Jewish roots, according to the Adam Sandler Ha-nukkah song, so that would be awesome if he showed up. But there's a cold going around. Three of the kids are out sick . . . so we're missing a couple of letters."

With a genuine smile, my first in days, I walk toward the stage to talk to Kimberly and the kids. "Thank you so much! That was so special. How did you learn that song?"

"Miss Atkinson taught us over lunch," one little red-headed girl says.

"We got extra cookies!" another boy adds.

"Bribery, huh?" I ask Noah, who shrugs and looks proud of himself as he high-fives a bunch of the kids. As he does, my stomach flips like tiny dreidels are spinning inside of it, mak-ing me dizzy, too. Crap. Seeing him with cute kids somehow makes him even more attractive, not that I would admit it to him, or myself. *Get in and get out, Hannah,* I tell myself. *No attachments.*

"Seriously. How did you pull that off?"

"Kim was my babysitter when I was younger. She was happy to help. Plus, I agreed to let the kids take a field trip to the deli to learn how to make bagels. It's a win-win for Jewish culture. I'm just saying. . . ."

We say good night to them and head toward the door as their parents start flooding out of the auditorium to pick them up, many of them saying hello to Noah and nodding at me politely but with interest. I guess because they know everyone in town and I'm an unfamiliar face.

When we're outside in front of the truck, Noah leans against it and his eyes search mine. "So how did I do?"

"The kids did a great job. I'll give you that," I say, meeting his eyes.

"And did they melt your cold, cold heart?" he asks with a grin.

"Who said my heart is cold? It's toasty warm when it comes to kids and stray dogs," I scoff as I go over to my side of the truck to open up my own door. "It was sweet, even if I don't usually do sweet. But there's no way you can keep this up for seven more nights. I stand undefeated. You can't top first graders singing 'The Dreidel Song.'"

"We'll see about that . . . ," Noah mutters as he starts the engine, turns the lights on, and heads back to my grandmother's. "You haven't seen anything yet. The magic has to last eight nights."

8

Night Two of Hanukkah

The reporter at the airport and the meteorologist standing outside on a Chicago street look as dejected as I feel. The reporter is standing in front of huge lines of angry, frustrated, and sad passengers stranded during the holidays. Meanwhile, the meteorologist looks like a human ice cream cone as the wind and snow buffet him from side to side.

"My best advice?" He turns to the camera, trying to pull his hat down over his bright red ears. "Stay home if you are in the path of the storm, and stay far away from the airports, wherever you are this week. That's it for me. Back to you, Bob," he says, wiping at his nose and trying to push the snow away, like he's unaware the camera is still rolling.

So one person is definitely worse off than I am—okay,

lots of people, judging by the folks in tears at the airport. Perspective is good, but it doesn't change the fact that I'm stuck here and I don't know for how long. No amount of singing elementary school students or charmingly cute deli workers is going to change that, even if Noah's getting under my skin in a somewhat good way.

As if I summoned them, my parents FaceTime me and pull me out of my confusing thoughts. The call immediately goes dead from a bad signal, so I go to another part of the house, closer to the window, and call them back.

"Happy Hanukkah, sweetie!" Mom's in her pajamas with a big cup of coffee on the kitchen table. She hands the phone over to my dad, who's already dressed in a sweater and jeans.

"Hi, honey!" he says.

They're awfully cheery for people who should be missing their daughter and upset she can't make it home.

"I guess you saw the news," Dad says. "It's rough out there. Flights are still being canceled and overbooked. People are camping out in the airport just to end up having to go back home anyway."

"We know you're disappointed, Hannah," my mom says. "You've always insisted on having a plan and sticking to it, no matter what. Even when you were little, you'd get upset if your routine was disrupted. We could never skip nap time or cut your sandwiches in different shapes. But this is a great lesson in flexibility. We'll celebrate whenever you get home. It will be like having two Hanukkahs!"

I sigh and roll my eyes, not caring that my mom doesn't like it. "I don't want two Hanukkahs. I just want one, where I'm supposed to be, and that doesn't involve cleaning horse stalls."

She hands the phone back to my dad, the voice of reason. "I understand. I do. But, unfortunately, your mom and I don't control the weather or the flight patterns. Neither do you. Part of getting older is learning to accept things that are out of our control. Only you can make the situation better for yourself. Make the most of it! Think of it as an adventure."

"I guess you have a point, but I reserve the right to be moody and annoyed in the meantime," I grumble.

"As opposed to your usual optimistic self." My mom raises an eyebrow.

"Fair enough," my dad agrees with me, and shoots my mom a look. "How about we call back tonight and light the candles together over the phone again."

I start to agree and hang up when I remember. "Actually, I have plans tonight."

"With your grandmother?" Mom asks. "She asked for my latke recipe." My mom made a face before hiding it in front of my dad since he doesn't like it when she critiques Nana's cooking, although he does it himself often enough.

"No. It's a long story, but Noah, Abe's grandson, is foisting his version of Hanukkah on me, hoping it's contagious. Like a rash. A huge, menorah-shaped rash."

My parents both burst out laughing. "I thought you loved Hanukkah," Mom says.

My dad pipes up, leaning closer to the screen. "You've

been so adamant about coming home because of it. Why not just enjoy it there this one time? It will be a great story to tell your friends."

He sounds just like my grandmother. I purse my lips. Even my own parents don't get it. "I love Hanukkah. I do! I love how we celebrate it in *New York,* with *our* family and friends. I love *our* traditions, which I can't do here. And our sometimes questionable latkes, and our special pan. None of that is here."

With a frown, my dad pushes up his glasses, which he always does when he's trying to think up an answer to a hard question, or the best way to frame his argument. Finally, he leans back toward the phone with a triumphant grin. "I think this will be good for you. Think of the actual Hanukkah story. Jews have had to adapt, to be flexible and create their own communities and traditions wherever they are. They've had to leave behind more than special pans. Think of the Passover story. . . ."

"Wrong holiday," my mom says. "You're getting off track."

I promise them I'll try because it's the fastest way to get off the phone. I know they think I'm being over dramatic, but it's not like I have that many holidays left with them before I go to college and everything changes. Sure, I may end up at NYU or Columbia, where I can easily get home, but what if I end up going elsewhere and moving farther away?

All I know is that Noah had better have a good plan for tonight to take my mind off snow cyclones and everything else.

As I'm getting ready for my shift at the deli, I stop in the kitchen, where my grandmother is straightening up. "Nana, are you sure it's okay if I go out again? We can stay here and play cards or something."

She studies my face like she's trying to decide what to say, then shakes her head. "It's okay, Hannah, we'll find some time to play cards later and you can tell me all about the deli when you get home."

She grabs her purse and leads me out to the car. She doesn't say anything else the rest of the way there, but I can't help feeling torn between wanting to spend more time with her and my promise to Noah.

About ten minutes later, we arrive at the deli. "I'll see you later, Nana," I say as she pats my hand and unlocks the car door. She gives me a small wave before driving away. I'm still looking in the direction of the departing car, wondering if I made the right choice, when Noah opens up the front door of the deli with a grin.

He's tight-lipped when I ask him about tonight, just smiling at me every once in a while. It's both infuriating and making me nervous. I asked him to step up his game. What if his game involves jumping out of a plane or performing in front of people, or something else I can't do?

Instead of worrying, I throw myself into work, wiping down counters, ringing up bagels, and talking up the food. "You should try the knishes, Mrs. Baker. Oh, how about I just add a couple of rugelach to your order? They're delicious. Do you like chocolate or apricot? Both? Both is good."

I catch Noah smiling at me. He gives me a thumbs-up, and my heart feels a little better. I may have a lousy Hanukkah, but I can still do something good for him and his grandfather if I can help save the deli. In a moment of inspiration, I take a video of the menorah made out of lox that Noah has created and post it on TikTok with a caption: *Blum & Sons made a Texas-sized menorah out of fish! #Texas #JewishFood #Holidays #Hanukkah.*

Later on in the day, I capture him holding a plate full of bagels and even twirling one on his finger. When things are quieter, he juggles a few. I laugh and record all of his antics on my phone. When he's distracted, I post a short video with a trending recording from the TikTok library. "I can't imagine a more beautiful thing."

And there's Noah serving bagels and twirling them with a giant smile meant just for me. Only, I want to share it with the world, to help save his business, so before I can overthink it, I make up a hashtag—#BagelBae—then include some others: #HotBagels, #JewishFood #SavetheDeli.

Satisfied, I smile to myself and post it, hoping it helps and he can thank me later.

I doubt *any* of my two hundred followers live close enough to come by, but you never know. At least I feel like I'm doing something helpful. Not knowing what his reaction would be, I don't show it to him, though. He has enough on his plate, literally, and figuratively, too.

He continues to smile at all the customers and at me, but

he has a very different look when he goes through the receipts periodically. The regulars, who I'm getting to know, are still coming in, but in smaller numbers. Noah notices this, too.

"I think people are freaked out by the weather, or they're trying to get out of town. We're normally busier than this," he says between customers. "The only good thing is that we'll be able to close early before tonight's festivities."

"I hope you aren't keeping the kids up after their bedtime again," I say, helping him stack the napkins in the holders and rearrange the take-out containers.

Noah gives me a brief grin. "No kids involved this time, but no hints either. I know what you're trying to do. Trust me, it will be worth it."

"I want to trust you." As I say it, I realize it's true, which is very odd. Noah's a bit of a disaster. Too impulsive, and cheery, and impossible to reason with, and yet, I do trust him and want him to succeed, so much so that I'm spending all this time working with him, just because he asked.

He pushes his longish hair out of his face and I study him out of the corner of my eye, when he's not looking. Something about him is growing on me, in a way that I didn't expect. Maybe it's because he keeps me off balance and helps me see things in a new light, or maybe like that itchy Hanukkah rash, his spirit is contagious after all. I can't help myself, and I grin at him but then put my face down and smother the smile. There's no reason he needs to know that I like him and that I could *really* like him, if I'd let myself. Because as soon as I can get a flight out, I need to take it.

But as I glance up again, he's looking at me like he saw my expression, and worse, read my heart, so I do what I do best and ignore it. "Okay," I say, putting on a businesslike tone. "I'm all done. Is there anything else to do, boss?"

He winces for a second at the cold emanating from me, but recovers quickly. "No. I think we're good here. Why don't we close up and head to our destination."

"Which is?" I ask. "I need to tell my grandmother what time I'll be home. I don't want her to worry . . . and she may need some help with the horses. Ringo seems to be limping a little since the storm."

Noah locks up the register, pats Mordechai, and turns the open sign to closed. "You worry too much. I've already been in touch with your grandmother. We have plenty of time."

He has an answer for everything, which makes it hard to argue. "How's your grandfather?" I ask.

"He's complaining about resting, but at least he's doing it. He's still coming in a few hours a day to prepare and cook, because he doesn't trust anyone but José and Consuela and himself to make everything, but at least he doesn't need to be on his feet all day serving and cleaning, and I'm going to make sure he takes all of Shabbat off."

"Good," I say. "I'm glad."

I follow him around the back of the building, but rather than wait for him to open the door, I jump in the truck myself, so as not to give him any ideas. He shakes his head but then gets into the driver's side without comment and hands me a shopping bag full of food and paper goods.

"What's this for?" I ask, considering we ate not too long ago.

"We're making a very special delivery," he says, and backs up, turning the radio on to some sad music without having to ask.

"Minor key, just like you like it," he jokes, but hums something more upbeat.

"Ha-ha," I say, but somehow it works, the sweet tune as a sort of counter melody to my own.

Along the way, he points out some things of interest that used to be there. "Here's where the first temple was, before they built the new one," he says, pointing to what is now a playground. "You can see the cemetery is still there. It was the first thing built by the Jewish community here, and it's still in use."

"Um, that's morbid, even for me." I glance over at the tombstones from the truck, some older-looking and some clearly newer.

Noah shrugs. "It's a permanent marker, a way of planting roots and saying we were here. It's pretty standard to build a cemetery, then a synagogue and mikvah, you know a ritual bath, and then Jewish businesses and community centers. Also houses."

"And now only the cemetery stands," I say. "And your deli."

"Exactly," he says, turning back to the road, then getting on a main road out of town. About twenty minutes later, we pull into what looks like a nursing home.

"What are we doing here?" I ask. "First kids, and now you're trying to lure me with cute elderly people?"

"Maybe." He grins. "I see how good you are with the customers. I figured you wouldn't mind. But first, you need to put this on," he says, handing me a second shopping bag he pulled out from the back seat. Inside is my very own ugly Hanukkah sweater, and it is super ugly. *Ugly* may not even do it justice. *Repulsive* is a better description. On a good day. It's even worse than the Christmas sweater the lady at the airport gave me, and that's saying a lot.

"No, thank you!" I say. "Happy to be here to play bingo or mah-jongg or whatever, but not wearing this."

"You promised you'd keep an open mind, Hannah," he says as he takes out his own sweater and puts it on over his T-shirt. As he does, his shirt rides up just enough that I can see part of his muscular stomach. I glance away before he catches me looking. He's even more attractive than he lets on behind the nice, goofy-guy facade, which isn't helping matters.

Blushing, I grab the bag back from him and furiously look down at the sweater again.

"I know you said you're sensitive to different materials, so this one is actually a cotton sweatshirt. I thought it would be better for you," he says in a deep, quiet voice by my ear.

I pull it out of the bag and see he's right. Don't get me wrong. It's still very ugly. Disco-themed menorahs and dreidels dance around the shirt, which reads *Give Me a Spin,* but at least it's soft cotton with a fleece-like interior. "Thank you," I say, grudgingly putting it on.

"Great!" He beams. "It brings some extra holiday cheer to the residents. This is the only Hanukkah party most of them get."

Carrying the shopping bag full of food, I follow him into the home, where he greets the person at the door, a sixty-something-year-old woman with a name tag that reads *Brenda*. "Howdy, Noah," she says. "Y'all can come right this way. They're waiting for you. In fact, they've been asking about you all week!"

Noah flashes her one of his famous smiles, clearly as comfortable here as anywhere else, then heads to what looks like a big community room. Residents are playing chess, Scrabble, reading, and talking to each other. Others seem less active but are being cared for by nurses and health care workers. A few people wave at him, and their eyes light up to see him. Whether they remember him or are just excited to have a visitor, I don't know, but it probably doesn't matter. Visiting the sick and elderly is a mitzvah for sure, and it makes me feel a little guilty for complaining so much about my own circumstances.

We make the rounds, saying hello to people. "This is Leora Bernstein," Noah says, introducing me. "She's Sol's cousin, so we go way back, right, ma'am?"

Mrs. Bernstein holds out a thin hand for me to shake. "He's never brought a young lady with him. You must be very special. . . ."

"Thank you, ma'am. I'm just visiting, but I'm happy to be here with y'all," I say, trying out the word on my own.

She laughs, and it's a musical little laugh. She must have been the belle of the ball when she was younger. "She's lovely for a Yankee, Noah. What a cute New York accent! You sound like my cousins who grew up in the Bronx. Can you say *y'all* again?"

Embarrassed, I comply. I guess, by trying to fit in, I didn't blend the way I thought I did.

Noah coughs or laughs. It's hard to tell, but Mrs. Bernstein winks at me. Clearly, elderly folks have some truth telling in common with kids. Delighted to see Noah off balance for once, I smirk, following him to set everything up for the party including banners, pictures of dreidels and menorahs, and trays of jelly doughnuts and small latkes that look a little different because they are low sodium and baked, not fried, according to Noah.

"Is everyone Jewish here?" I ask him quietly, realizing that the residents are of different backgrounds and ethnicities. Of course, there are lots of Jews of Color, especially in New York, but maybe not as many here. Although considering the story he told me about crypto Jews like Consuela's family, there's a lot I don't know about Texan Jewish history.

"No. The place started out as a home for Jewish seniors, but anyone can live here. Since my grandfather was younger, we've always hosted a Hanukkah party for the residents, which is one of my favorite things of the year. It's kind of our way of giving back. Sure, we could just drop off the food, but it means more to visit and celebrate with them. Do you know what I mean?"

I swallow and look up at him but can only nod. Noah may be impulsive and a little ridiculous, but I don't know if I've met anyone like him before. As I open my mouth to say something, he starts passing out napkins to each resident sitting down and motions for me to carry the tray of doughnuts over so he can pass those out, too.

"My doctor says I'm not supposed to have sugar," one of the residents says before I get to him.

"Don't worry, Mr. Cohen, I have a special, plain doughnut that's sugar free just for you," Noah says, going back to the table and picking up a brown paper bag that's been set aside. "Just like last year." He winks at me, and I can't help it. I get as gooey inside as the sugary treats I'm holding.

I'm not sure I'm going to make it through all eight nights of this without falling for Noah. I can already feel the armadillo-strength shell I've put around my heart start to soften, and to be absolutely honest, it scares the Hanukkah lights right out of me.

When Noah's done dividing the treats and all the residents are happily chatting and noshing, he turns to me with a grin. "I know you haven't had a chance to light the candles with your community this year, so I thought I'd lend you my community."

He pulls out an electric menorah from the bag. "Sorry, they don't let me light candles here. Too many oxygen tanks."

"Yeah, that would be bad. . . ."

The menorah is one of those ivory plastic ones you can get

at CVS at home. It's not pretty at all, yet my eyes water a bit as we both climb under the table, because a menorah doesn't have to be pretty to be meaningful. I reach over to help him plug it in behind the big folding table against the wall. As we do, my hand brushes his for a second and instantly heats up like there's a real flame in the plastic candle holder. But no, there's no fire. There's only Noah.

He must feel it, too, because his eyes open wide and he licks his lips as if his mouth is dry or as if he wants to kiss me right there, under the table of the community room in the Jewish senior home. But in an instant, the moment passes as one of the residents yells out something about what beautiful Jewish babies we'd make, maybe thinking we can't hear her, or maybe she doesn't care. I can't wait to be eighty and not have a filter.

Although, what the heck! Babies? I'm only seventeen years old! I want to say but don't, out of respect and a whole lot of embarrassment. Plenty of people their age met and married high school sweethearts, so maybe they don't mean right away, but down the line.

Blushing furiously, I go to stand up and, forgetting I'm under a table, bump my head, then have to crawl out on my hands and knees. Not exactly the most dignified I've ever looked. I turn and Noah looks dazed, too, but he seems to recover and holds out a hand to help me out. Again, I can't figure out if this is a polite Texan thing or if it's just him, and us. Despite not knowing, I take his warm hand and stand up beside him, forgetting the gaggle of seniors in the room with us until Noah clears his throat and the moment has passed, for better or for worse.

"Do you want to do the honors?" Noah asks me, gesturing toward the menorah.

"Sure!" I say brightly, maybe too brightly, because it even sounds fake to my ears, but I don't have time to obsess over my tone of voice, as twenty senior citizens are looking at me with anticipation. Taking a deep breath, I turn toward the menorah. First I twist the shamash, the lead candle, and then I sing the blessings as I light the first two candles for the first two nights, chanting the Hebrew from memory and reading the English off a sheet Noah put on the table from HIAS, a Jewish nonprofit organization that helps refugees. "Baruch atah Adonai Eloheinu Melech ha-olam, asher kid'shanu b-mitzvotav, v-tzivanu l'hadlik ner shel Hanukkah. Blessed are you, Our God, Ruler of the Universe, who makes us holy through Your commandments, and commands us to light the Hanukkah lights."

As I begin the second blessing, I notice that the voices behind me are getting stronger. I imagine them remembering, deep in their bones and in their souls, saying and singing these prayers out loud with their own families throughout the years, and now I am openly teary. Not from grief from missing my family, but from something else, like a profound gratitude to be able to share this moment with them, to be part of the tradition that goes back centuries or l'dor v'dor. From generation to generation.

"Baruch atah Adonai Eloheinu Melech ha-olam, she-asah nisim la-avoteinu v-imoteinu ba-yamim ha-heim ba-z'man ha-zeh. Blessed are you, Our God, Ruler of the Universe, who performed miracles for our ancestors in their days at this season."

I wipe at my eyes quickly, trying to hide it, but I feel Noah's hand on my back. This touch is different from the other one, under the table, because it's intentional and steady, meant to comfort me or to acknowledge the profound moment we're in together. I glance up at him, and he smiles for one second and studies my face, as if he's studying it or seeing it for the very first time.

But then he lets go and takes in the room again. "Well, folks, I think it's time for a couple of songs. I hear my friend Hannah here loves 'I Have a Little Dreidel.' Who wants to help make Hannah's Hanukkah dreams come true?"

"Aren't they cute together?" Mrs. Bernstein says to the woman next to her, loudly. The woman shushes her, but Noah just grins and launches into the song. Those who can sing, sing loudly and with gusto. Those who can clap, clap, and soon, even the nurses and health care workers are clapping and laughing.

It's not the New York City Hanukkah I'm used to, but in this antiseptic-smelling, ugly linoleum-floored room, under the florescent lights, with this boy, I experience something special that I won't soon forget.

Catching Noah's eyes as he dances with an older woman with a cane, I have a feeling he won't be able to forget it either.

Night Three of Hanukkah

The weather is on in the background, but I don't even notice. I'm not looking at the flight cancellations or anything else as I drink my coffee, eat a granola bar, and throw on sneakers. After last night, I'm suddenly in less of a rush to get home than I was. At least right now.

"I'll go check the horses before my shift at the deli," I tell my grandmother. If she seems surprised, she doesn't say anything. Out of the corner of my eye, I catch her smile into her mug, though.

"I'll take you to work in thirty minutes, Hannah," she says, standing to rinse off the breakfast dishes. "Although I do wish you'd take some time and relax with me. I didn't bring you here just to work. This is supposed to be a break for you.

I know how hard you've been working in school and with all your volunteering."

"Thanks, Nana," I say, surprised and a little touched that she knows I've been volunteering as a reading tutor at the community center a few days a week. "You know what, I bet Noah can wait a bit for help. Why don't we have another cup of coffee and play a few hands of cards?"

I sink down into a seat at the kitchen table as she pours me a cup and puts out a few slices of coffee cake on a plate with a wink. I've already had breakfast, but I dig in anyway.

"When you were little you used to like Go Fish," she says, digging out a pack of cards from a drawer in the kitchen. "What's your game of choice these days?"

"Well, I promised Josh I'd fully experience Texas, so maybe some Texas Hold'em poker?" I shuffle the cards and make a bridge like my dad taught me, then deal as my grandmother beams.

"You know, I taught your dad that trick. He's not a great card player, but his shuffling intimidates people and helps him bluff. . . ."

"I knew it! He always acts like he has good cards and I end up folding. I'll have to use that to my advantage next time. . . ."

We laugh and play a few rounds before I glance up at the clock and wince. Now I'm really late. Eating the last bite of coffee cake, I clear my plate and then dash into the barn.

After making sure Ringo and Paul have enough water and hay and that the stalls are fairly clean, I'm on my way up to the shower, taking two stairs at a time. In the shower, I hum to myself and smile now that no one is looking, imagining what Noah has planned for today. Cute Jewish dogs? What else could top kids and seniors?

In New York, I let my guard down at home and with friends, but you have to have an impersonal mask on when out in public, as a defense. You can't be open, because open is vulnerable.

Here, I start to feel my mask melting just a little bit. I feel somehow a tad lighter, but yeah, afraid of being a different kind of vulnerable, because what happens when I leave here? Whether it's tomorrow or in a few days, or even next week, getting close to people means it's easier to get hurt, to go off track. My track has been set for a long time. Get into college, choose one, leave for college and focus on that. I can't afford to get distracted at this point.

But for now, all I can focus on is seeing Noah again. One shift and one night of Hanukkah at a time.

When I'm dried off and ready, just like the dreidel in the song, I'm back downstairs, patting Elvis and waiting for my grandmother to emerge. In a few minutes, she does, with her purse in hand and a leash for the dog, who is now officially hers since the shelter located his owners, an elderly couple who were thrilled that my grandmother wanted to adopt him.

"I have to take him everywhere because he gets separation anxiety when I'm not home," she says, leading us both to the truck.

I glance at Elvis's big, round eyes and waggy tail, and I understand the separation anxiety. It's kind of like me when I first arrived in Texas a few days ago. It's still not home, and I still miss my family, my bagel cart, and my friends and our annual ski trip, but Rosenblum's charms have crept up on me, for sure. Although that may be one five-foot-ten boy-shaped charm in particular.

I know I've thought Noah is ridiculous more than a few times, but now I'm being the ridiculous one, getting all worked up over a guy I've only known a few days, and who I probably won't see again.

I climb into the passenger side as the dog gets in the back seat. "So what's on the menu today?" Nana asks. "Anything special?" She's drumming her fingers again, but this time she seems more relaxed. The frost is gone, the roads are clear, and there are more cars out and about. I think our card game was good for her, too. Good for both of us, really. She waves at a few of her neighbors, who wave back from their yards or their own vehicles.

"I'm not sure. I know Noah was planning something for Hanukkah, but I don't know what it is. You probably know more than I do. Can you give me a hint? I won't tell him!" I ask in a rush, wondering why I didn't think to pry information from her before.

She just laughs. "I meant on the actual menu, but I guess I know where your mind is these days, and why you didn't even ask me about your flight this morning. It's still backed up by the way. I'll let you know if I hear any more from your parents."

I duck my head, trying not to blush. If I'm that obvious to my grandmother, I need to pull myself together before going to work. I'm not sure I want Noah to think I care that much. He may be impulsive and the kind of guy who flirts with everyone he meets, but I definitely am not. Plus, I still have a bet on the line, and another five nights of Hanukkah, not to mention a flight out of town at some point.

My grandmother pulls in front of the deli, and I give her a quick kiss without thinking. She looks pleased as I jump out of the truck. Elvis cries for a second until I reach into the open window and pat him on the head, too.

Once I'm out of the truck, I notice something. There's an actual line of people waiting at the counter, not just our usual locals. Noah is beaming, but also moving quickly, like someone sped up a video of a baseball player. He's everywhere all at once, behind the counter, pouring coffee, grabbing pastry, and ringing up customers.

For a second, I feel guilty for being so late, but spending time with my grandmother is important, too, and if anyone would get that, Noah would.

While Noah in action is adorable and a little comical, I tear myself away from the image in order to go help, walking around the counter, putting on my apron and heading behind the cash register. "Sorry I'm late!" I say to him before addressing the next customer. "Good morning, ma'am. What can we get for you?" I say to the fifty-something woman in black leggings, black boots, and a funky scarf, not the deli's usual clientele from what I've gathered.

She pulls up her phone. "I'm just passing through on an antiquing trip, but my daughter said to stop by here. She saw a TikTok about it. What do you recommend?"

My eyes widen and glance over to Noah, who looks equally as shocked. Someone saw my video and shared it. What if the other people in line found us the same way? I guess it's possible, if not probable. I don't have a chance to think about it, because I'm babbling about different kinds of spreads, pastries, and sandwiches, and soon she's leaving with a big bag of food and we're even running out of certain things.

That's when I start to panic. "Noah!" I pull him aside right after I sell the last loaf of challah about fifteen minutes later. "What if we run out?"

He grins. "That's even better. In Texas, that's the mark of a successful business. Lots of barbeque places even advertise that they'll serve until they sell out every day. It drives more customers and makes the place seem like there's a greater demand. If you have food left at the end of the day, it means your place isn't doing as well. We can just do that! It's a Texas tradition!"

The next two hours are a whirlwind of me posting signs on the door about what we've run out of and letting customers know to come back earlier the next day. I manage to snap a few photos of lines and happy customers, and in a moment of inspiration, I realize that if TikTok can bring in more customers, maybe we can take it even further and use it to fundraise to save the deli. When we have a lull and Noah's in the kitchen, I quickly start a GoFundMe page and create a short video.

"Hey, bagel enthusiasts! If you love Jewish food and Texas charm, please, please help us save this slice of Texas Jewish history! Blum and Sons means so much to so many in the community. It's a family-run business that's stood here for generations. Visit! Spread the word so we can spread the lox! And donate what you can to help an awesome family serve great food!"

I save the video but don't get a chance to post it because Noah comes back and we have more customers.

By 3:00 p.m., we are out of enough food that we have to close, four whole hours early. I draw up a fresh sign, and Noah turns the open sign to closed on the front door, pulling the blinds down as well.

"Now what?" I ask, sinking into a vinyl booth and putting my head down on the cool linoleum. "I'm not sure I'm up for anything wild tonight."

"Me neither." Noah slides into the booth across from me. "I don't know how my grandfather does this at his age. Granted, he doesn't usually have as many customers. Or has to answer questions about the menu over and over." As if remembering something, he stands up and goes over to the cooler to pull out a couple of seltzers, then walks slowly back to the table. Even Noah, with his endless energy, is drained from the hectic day, it seems.

Handing me a drink, he holds out his in a toast. "To Hannah, who helped make this all possible, and who knows her way around a good pickle. L'chaim!"

"To Noah, who makes an awesome grilled cheese but still hasn't convinced me of the magic of his version of Hanukkah. I'm just saying. . . ." I hold out my own can of seltzer, but he winces at my backhanded compliment.

Maybe it was a little mean, but I'm not ready to give up on our Hanukkah experiment now that his business is doing well. He promised me Hanukkah magic.

I bite my lip and realize that it's more than that. I still want to see him outside of work but can't admit it. Not yet. At least not until I know he feels the same way.

Noah gulps down the rest of the seltzer, then tosses the can in the recycling bin. "You're right. One night of magic coming up. Luckily, I planned ahead and this one doesn't involve rigorous activity."

I glance down at my now-stained T-shirt and leggings.

Noah just holds out his hand for my apron and takes off his as well, hanging them both on the hook behind the counter. His hair is messy, and his own Blum and Sons shirt is in as bad shape as mine, but he doesn't seem bothered.

Rather he holds out his hand to help me out of the booth. His hand is warm, his long fingers slightly calloused from all the work in the kitchen. Once we touch for real, not just by accident, I feel it. *Magic.* I drop my hand right away and scramble behind him, wiping my hand on my leggings, trying to pretend I didn't feel anything out of the ordinary.

"Don't worry, where we're going is dark and I doubt anyone else will see us."

Uttered by practically anyone else that would sound pretty

creepy, but considering Noah made me take a spider out of the kitchen rather than killing it, I'm not all that worried. If spiders are safe around him, I'm assuming I am, too.

"I hope they won't smell us either," I say, before I realize that I'm probably not supposed to comment on either one of us smelling like fried potatoes. Normal girls wouldn't mention that on a date, if that's what this is. I can't be sure, and I don't want to ask.

We exit the back door, since the front is closed already, and head toward the courtyard, but rather than go toward his truck he beckons me forward. "We can walk there," he says, stuffing his hands in his jeans pockets, either out of embarrassment or maybe regret that he touched me before. Maybe it was the opposite of magical for him. Or my reaction was too weird. Or maybe it was crossing a line we both drew up and didn't need to cross. New York and Texas are awfully far away, so it's probably easier to just be friendly coworkers/kinda friends for the next few days.

I make sure to give him some space when we walk. Other than a few small restaurants, everything is already closed in the square already. The small lights on the awnings and in the store windows twinkle. It's a huge difference from New York, where something is always open and people are always around. And yet, the quiet and solitude are peaceful, like we have the place entirely to ourselves.

We walk toward the gazebo, and that's when I see it. Next to the Christmas tree in the center of town is a big menorah, lit up in blue lights outlining it. The first three candles and the shamash are lit.

"But how?" I ask, looking back at Noah. "This wasn't here yesterday."

Noah's face is transformed by a huge smile as I run toward the menorah and circle around it.

"It looks just like the one at Lincoln Center!"

When I get to the front of it, I feel him standing behind me, close enough that I can feel his breath on my neck.

"It's the menorah from the old synagogue's front lawn," he explains. "I had to make a bunch of calls to track it down, and tie it down in my truck, but it was worth it. You haven't seen the best part yet," he says. "Look at the sign."

It's dark where the plaque is, even with the lights of the menorah and Christmas tree illuminating the sign. So I take out my phone and turn on the flashlight.

In small letters it says *Dedicated to the members of the Jewish community of Rosenblum, past and present.*

"My buddy Colin's dad works at the office supply store a few towns over. He made this for me. Laminated it and everything so it will be okay in the weather."

I turn quickly, and Noah is right there. The ground is uneven, so I start to slip, until he holds on to me with two hands on my arms, glancing down at me with anticipation. I lick my lips to say something, and he leans in but then hesitates. "So what do you think? Do you like it? No cute kids, no adorable seniors. No dogs in Hanukkah sweaters, although I'll have to try that one someday. Just the quiet and serious holiday you always wanted."

"I love it," I say softly. "It's majestic."

"And magical?" he asks hopefully, but takes a step back like he's second-guessing being so close to me.

I put my hands on his arms in return and glance up at his perfect mouth, which isn't smirking or smiling, or showing any of Noah's other usual expressions. This one is different, somehow less sure, less impulsive, and more thoughtful. I'm seriously contemplating closing the distance between us and kissing him. My entire being wants to kiss him to thank him for tonight, for the promise of tomorrow, and for a million other reasons. My heartbeat quickens, nerves and excitement making me take shallow breaths, as I debate closing my eyes and hoping he will take the hint or keeping them open so I can see his reaction.

But before I overthink everything further, a car pulls into the lot and interrupts us with a loud beep. Flushed, I step back and push my hair behind my ears, right before slipping on the wet grass and landing on my behind. This, this is my fate, just like my mom says in Yiddish, "Man plans and God laughs."

"Ouch!" I yelp, then put my head in my hands, certain I'm the color of Noah's deep red borscht soup he was experimenting with the other day.

That's what I get for thinking about kissing him moments after I decided we should just be friends. Somewhere God is having a big chuckle at my expense.

Noah groans as the voices of three loud elderly men start

yelling over each other. "Sol, it's beautiful! Oh, Irving, look at that. We haven't had a menorah that big, ever. Other than the one at the temple. I'm all verklempt."

"It *is* the one from the synagogue," Abe says, the last voice to chime in. "Noah, come help us up the hill. We have some treats to celebrate."

Noah holds out his hand again but looks torn as his grandfather calls to him. "It's okay. I can get up by myself." The only thing hurt is my dignity. What if they hadn't arrived in time? Would I have actually done it? Kissed Noah and made the first move?

I bite my lip knowing the truth. I absolutely would have. And judging from how he's looking back at me, I'm pretty sure he'd be more than okay with it. I just don't know if either one of us would regret it later.

I dust off the dirt and grass from my jeans and slowly make my way down the little hill to help bring up the treats and the older men. All along the way they're chatting about their grandchildren who saw our message on TikTok and heard we sold out of food today.

"What is this TikTok? Is it a watch you wear?" Abe asks, and Sol launches into a description of a documentary he saw about the dangers of social media. "And that's why people are so lonely, and why they don't know how to have conversations anymore, or date. Right? Of course I'm right. We should go back to writing letters. I still have all the letters my Sophie wrote me. May her memory be a blessing. Noah, are you on this social media thing?"

"Nope, I'm more of a flip-phone guy," Noah says, taking his phone from his pocket and showing it to them. "I can call and text, but that's about it. I find it freeing. It makes me more present, you know?"

"Smart boy . . . ," Sol says. "You always had a good head on your shoulders."

"Well, I don't know about whether social media is to blame for what's wrong with the world," Abe says, "but I'm proud of these two kids for coming up with a way to reach new customers. A Hanukkah miracle!"

"But will the gefilte fish last eight days?" Irv asks with a wink.

"No one under seventy eats gefilte fish," Abe says. "Which is a shame."

"It's all Hannah," Noah says modestly, but I know the truth, which is that part of the draw was the video I did of him making and serving food, and calling him Bagel Bae. Plenty of young girls and guys on TikTok saw immediately what took me a while to see, that Noah is irresistible. The question is, how long can I resist him myself? Judging by how I almost threw myself at him, I have my answer. Not long enough.

Once we're up the hill and sitting in the gazebo with the light of the menorah nearby, the men pull out some seltzer and doughnuts to share. I've had too much of both those items already for at least the next week, so I politely decline and gesture to Noah. Taking the hint, he stands up and hugs and kisses his grandfather on the cheek and hugs the other two men. "I better see Hannah home. Y'all have a good night and a happy Hanukkah."

I wave goodbye, but the three men surround me with a hug as well. It's not family, well, not my own family, but I see what makes his small community mean so much to Noah. There's a sense that since there are so few Jews left, they have formed their own family, spanning decades and generations.

We walk back to the deli, me struggling to keep up with Noah's long legs, and slightly limping after my fall. He pushes his floppy hair out of his face. "I'm sorry about that. I didn't expect them."

Is he sorry that they interrupted us or sorry about something else? I don't ask because I'm not sure I want the answer. Now that we didn't kiss, I remember all the reasons we shouldn't. "That's okay. They're a hoot! And clearly, the menorah means so much to them, too. I didn't know you never had a public one. I'm so impressed that you managed to pull that off so quickly."

He grins for real. "Yeah, despite what my dad says, I can be organized when I have to. It turns out the mayor used to be my history teacher, so all I had to do was provide him with some documents about the Jewish community and founders of the town. Plus figure out where the menorah was stored. He asked me to work with some local historians to create something more permanent, too. Because this will have to come down in a few weeks. It's not meant to handle the Texas summer."

I nod. "So maybe something else good has come out of this."

Noah clears his throat, something he seems to do when he's nervous. "Other than the obvious?"

"What's the obvious?" I ask, swallowing hard and willing him to say it.

But rather than using his words, he takes my hands in his, and this time there's no mistaking it. He's touching me on purpose, because he wants to, not because he's helping me up or by accident. I entangle my hands with his, because it feels right here with Noah, who is trying so hard to make me feel at home. It isn't home, but here with him, I feel more like myself, or what I could be, than I thought possible.

I look up at him, and he bites the corner of his lip before pushing a curl behind my ear. "This is the best thing to come out of our Hanukkah experiment. By far."

And without another word, I do what I should have done earlier, what I'd been secretly wanting to do for the past three days, despite my efforts to keep my distance from Noah. He's my opposite in almost every way, but maybe not in the ways that matter because he's what my grandmother would call a "good egg" and my heart is getting more and more scrambled by him by the day.

I throw my arms around his neck so his mouth meets mine and I kiss him with all the pent-up frustration, delight, and mishmash of confusing emotions that swirl around my head until there's just one prevailing thought in my mind.

How much I want to kiss him and that I hope he wants to kiss me back just as much.

Noah's lips start out soft as they cover mine gently, first kissing my top lip and then my bottom one. I press mine against his, a little firmer, and he makes a slightly surprised but encouraging *mm* sound as I put my hands on the back of his neck, to bring him down to me so I can reach him better.

Noah happily obliges, scooping me up in his arms, playing with my hair, nipping gently at my lips, and then his kisses grow more insistent, like he's trying to convince me of something, but he doesn't have to. I'm already fully convinced. There's nothing I'd rather be doing, or anywhere else I'd rather be than kissing this adorable boy, here on the third night of Hanukkah.

10

Night Four of Hanukkah

Noah picks me up for work this morning, eliciting a raised eyebrow from my grandmother, and a quick smile from me, which makes his even wider. As soon as Nana is out of earshot, he leans over and says softly, "You know you're beautiful when you smile. You should do it more often."

I narrow my eyes and flatten my lips, the exact opposite of smiling, but he raises his hands to apologize. "Not trying to be one of those jerks who tells women to smile. I just wanted to tell you that happy looks good on you."

My face relaxes. "Okay, well, thank you. I guess I'll take that in the spirit it's meant."

He even has a jar of pickles wrapped up in a bow for me. "The flower shop is closed this early."

"Oh, please, I'd much rather have pickles. Flowers die. Why would you give someone something that's already been torn from its life force, like flowers?"

"Morose, isn't it? Like love dies, too? But I thought you liked morose." He laughs. "I, on the other hand, like flowers. They're a reminder that we have to enjoy fleeting moments of beauty."

I shrug. "I like pickles. Pickles are forever."

He grins. "See, pickles times happiness equals smiles squared."

I roll my eyes and go to put them on the counter.

"What? Einstein was Jewish. I'm sure he liked a good pickle, too," Noah says.

My grandmother laughs at the gift but pushes us out the door with a promise to stop by around lunch if we have any food left.

Sure enough, she stops by the deli at one o'clock, and Noah dashes out from behind the counter to give her the VIP treatment at a booth while she looks equal parts amused and impressed, winking at me when he turns his back.

"Mrs. Levin, please, I insist that lunch is on us. You've been so nice to my grandfather by letting us monopolize Hannah that it's the least we can do." Noah brushes away her attempt to pay.

She shakes her head and throws some money in a tip jar when he isn't looking, then gives me a quick hug before shooting me a knowing glance and exiting the deli. She doesn't have to say anything more to show that she approves of me spending time with Noah. He has that effect on everyone, especially me.

It's a wonder we manage to sell anything, considering how flustered I am all day and how distracted Noah is. I can't stop staring at his forearms, strong from work, and yes, his mouth, which kissed me last night, or let me kiss him, depending on how you look at it. Considering this morning, I think he liked it as much as I did, but there's only one way to be sure, which is to do it again as soon as possible.

Unfortunately, we have several hours of work in the way before we're alone.

When the line of customers goes down, I run to the bathroom and splash some cold water on my face. Luckily, despite our clumsiness, and awkwardness, we sell out even quicker today and manage to close the doors at 2:45, fifteen minutes earlier than yesterday.

"Phew!" I say as he shuts the door and puts up the closed sign. Either we're getting used to handling so many customers or we're excited about being alone together, but neither one of us seems as tired as we were yesterday.

Noah takes three long strides toward me and lifts me up, swinging me around. He may be lanky, but I can feel some serious muscles in his arms when he puts me down. "Where did we leave off?" I ask, swallowing hard, willing him to kiss me again, but he just gives me a quick peck next to my lips and leads me toward the kitchen.

"Tonight, I thought I'd give you a special lesson," he says, picking me up again and placing me on top of the industrial steel counter, which is cool under my legs and hands, a welcome contrast to the rest of me, which is warm from working and, yeah, from just being near Noah, who radiates heat in every glance he gives me.

"Um, what kind of lesson?" I ask, focusing in on his lips and wondering if I could teach him a thing or two as well. All I know is that I'd like to try.

He shakes his head and pulls out a giant pan and bowl. "My family's secret latke recipe. I literally had to clear it with my grandfather to share this with you. You need to promise not to leak it to Katz's or any other Jewish deli back home. I'm serious about that. I'm actually surprised he isn't making you sign a nondisclosure form. It's been in the family for generations, but as an official employee of Blum's, you've earned it."

"I promise," I say, holding up my hand in Spock's "live long and prosper" salute.

"That's not the Girl Scout Promise," he says, wagging a spatula at me.

"I was never a Girl Scout, but I am a *Star Trek* fan and Leonard Nimoy made up the salute based on a Jewish priestly blessing, so I figured it was better." I shrug. "More fitting for the occasion, too."

"Fine." Noah leans over for a quick peck on my lips this time but lingers for a second. "It will do. I trust you." His eyes tell a different story than the playful expression on his lips. His eyes tell me that he means what he says in all sincerity. He does trust me, with his recipe, his family business, and maybe more.

I gulp and look away, unable to deal with the weight of the responsibility, and the truth, which is that I trust him, too. Noah is so much more than the impulsive, sugar-eating Chaos Muppet I thought he was at first, no matter what his dad says. Noah just needs to see it for himself, because beneath his swagger, he has doubts. I can sense it when he's not hiding them. It's like he feels he needs to be on, entertaining all the time, that he's not enough. Not smart enough, responsible enough, or whatever rubbish his dad has been telling him to try to get him to fit in with his expectations.

But I see the real him and know that he's more than enough. At least for me. He's also more than enough for this town and should think about broadening his horizons. That's one thing his dad and I agree on, not that I would tell Noah that he should consider going away to a bigger town or city, or really anywhere beyond Rosenblum. He's wasted here when there's a whole world that could use his energy and his ridiculous optimism.

In a flash, Noah is back to his normal self. "Now, my grandfather already peeled and shredded a few potatoes for us, so we don't have to do the hard stuff. However, when you shred yourself, be careful because you can scrape your skin and that hurts like heck. Plus, blood is not the taste we're going for. . . . It's totally not kosher." He holds out his hands for me to inspect the small burns, scrapes, and calluses, but rather than warn me off, they just make me like him more. These are hands that care and take care of his grandfather, of me when I fell, and of so many others. In fact, I've never seen more perfect hands.

But I just nod. "Point taken. More oil, less blood. Animal sacrifice went out of fashion a couple thousand years ago."

He grins. "Exactly. With the second temple, if I remember correctly. Now, the trick of the oil is to get a good amount in there and keep it at the perfect temp. Not too hot, but hot enough. Oh, and you need to drain all the water from the potatoes with a clean towel or else they won't cook well. It looks like my grandfather did that already, too. . . . He must have wanted us to get to the good stuff. . . ."

"What good stuff?" I ask, leaning in for another kiss. "This?"

"The cooking, Hannah, I was talking about cooking. My grandfather likes you, but I doubt he is thinking about anything but cooking."

"Uh-huh," I said, pretending I knew that.

He continues with his tips, but I'm only half listening because I'm so intrigued with him and his command of the kitchen, the way he holds the pan, flips the latkes, and the way his eyebrows knit together in concentration when he plates the potato pancakes perfectly. It's mesmerizing and captivating to watch him in his element, doing what he loves. He's good at it, too, especially for someone so young. I watch enough cooking shows that I can tell he's the real deal, passionate about food, charismatic, and talented.

In the kitchen, he's someone else. He's not goofy or

impulsive. He's serious and confident, and I could watch him all day.

Normally, I'm a great student, but here, I can't help focusing on the teacher rather than the subject, until he puts down the pan and holds out his arms to help me off the counter. "Now you try," he says, facing me toward the pan.

"Um, that's okay. I'd much rather watch you and eat your efforts," I say, tilting my head back toward him for a kiss.

He grants it to me with a smirk but then wraps my hands around the pan handle, close enough behind me that he can whisper. "But don't you want to impress your friends and family and the cranky woman in apartment seven B who told you to get frozen latkes? Heck, even the fire department will be impressed if you don't have to call them next year."

I sigh, partially because he's so close to me, and partially because he's absolutely right. I'm competitive enough that I do want to learn and no longer have to have the smoke alarm alert the neighbors of our failures.

"Fine. Teach me everything, chef."

Noah carefully puts a heap of potatoes, onions, and secret spices on the hot pan, takes one of my hands in his bigger hand, and smushes the potato down with the spatula until it is about an inch and a half deep and round. I don't know if it's the heat from his hand or the pan, but I'm suddenly flushed. Who knew that making latkes is perfect for flirting? Not me. But when he helps my hand flip them, my stomach flips right along with them. When the latkes are on the plate and he cuts into a hot fried pancake and feeds me a small bite, dipping it in sour cream like I like it, more than my mouth is on fire. My heart is, too. That's when I know, over the plate of potato latkes in a deli kitchen in a small town in Texas, of all places. I glance at Noah and can't look away.

The feeling comes out of nowhere, like the hora at my cousin's wedding—loud, fast, disorientating, and one hundred precent inevitable. I love Noah. Only, I'm not sure what to do with that knowledge, other than keep it to myself. For both of our sakes. No matter what, I still have to leave town and he needs to stay. No good can come out of a love confession from me.

I chew and swallow the pancake, and of course, it's the best thing I've ever eaten in my life because it nourishes more than my stomach and my basic needs. It tastes like our shared history and like our present, familiar and exciting at the same time.

"Good?" he asks, running his thumb over my lip where a bit of sour cream was smeared.

"You can say that," I answer, licking my lip before he captures it in yet another kiss, which is as sweet as the applesauce he's eaten, but it's more than that. It's him. Noah embodies sweetness. He's like a double dose of apples and honey on Rosh Hashanah. Sweeter than sweet and a promise of good things to come.

"I love them," I finally say, because it's the closest I can come to the truth.

I never thought anything could distract me from something as delicious as these perfectly round, crisp latkes, but it turns out, I had never met anyone like Noah before, someone who makes me question everything, see everything in a new light, and someone who is absolutely nothing like what I thought I wanted.

He whirls me away from the hot pan and plates toward the fridge, which he leans me against. The cool surface is a relief after being over the stove.

"I'm going to save setting the kitchen on fire and having to call the firemen for another night, if that's okay. They're awfully handsome in this town, and I don't want the competition, to be honest."

"More than okay," I whisper, and am about to kiss him again when footsteps approach and we each take a step back from each other like kids caught doing, well, exactly what we were doing.

Noah's grandfather turns on a few more lights. "I don't know how you cook in the dark. You'll strain your eyes," he says, before going to the island in the center of the kitchen to inspect our efforts.

"Good, good. My grandson's quite the talent, don't you think, Hannah? This place will be in good hands with him when I finally retire. Whenever that is. I'm trying to hold on until he's ready."

Looking right at Noah, still flushed from kissing and cooking, I have to agree. "He's quite something, for sure."

Night Five of Hanukkah

My grandmother bursts into my bedroom the next morning and opens the lace curtains. "Great news, Hannah Banana! Your parents just called. They managed to get you a seat on a flight on Sunday. A lot of people don't want to fly on Christmas Eve, so it was the only day they could find something that wasn't eight hundred dollars or a standby seat. They even managed to upgrade you to a window seat!"

I sit up in bed, and the harsh light hits my face like a harsher dose of reality. "Oh, okay. Thanks. I guess."

My grandmother purses her lips, seemingly confused. "I thought you'd be thrilled. You can make it home in time for the last night of Hanukkah with your parents. Josh will be there, too, and you mom even said something about inviting your friends over and ordering Chinese food and streaming a movie. Isn't that what you wanted?"

I flop back on my pillow and sigh. "Yeah. Exactly what I wanted." A few days ago. Now I'm not sure I'm ready to say goodbye, or if I'll be ready in three days or even three months. I want to finish what I've started with Noah, but I can't explain that to my parents or my grandmother after I've complained for days, so I get up, swing my legs off the bed, and paste on a grim smile.

"Thanks again for the news. And for letting me stay here all this time."

I grab her for an impromptu hug, something I wouldn't have done a week before I arrived and she felt more or less like a stranger. Now I breathe in her warm scent of coffee, mixed with leather from the saddles and horse shampoo, and hug her tight, before letting go and starting to head for the shower for some time to think.

Before I start the water, Becky texts in our group chat. *Tell your mom to order extra dumplings. Should we invite Max?* she asks, referring to a cute guy I met through youth group a couple months ago.

I'm about to text back right away but then pause before hitting send. To be honest, I can barely recall what Max is like, other than a pale comparison to Noah. The main thing he has going for him is that he's in New York, where I'll be soon, too.

Noah may be amazing. He probably is, but how can I put my life on hold for someone I've only known a few days who I may never see again after this week? I frown at myself, feeling as ambivalent as a black-and-white cookie from Eli's. I have one foot in each place, Texas and New York. Worse, my heart is split as well, and I only have one.

Sure.

It's not a full-throated yes, but it means I'm open to the possibility, or I hope I will be by the time I have to leave Noah behind.

I jump in the shower for real and try to wash away that ambivalence, that torn feeling about not feeling like I belong here but not wanting to leave either. Unfinished business, or an unresolved plot. I always hate cliff-hangers or ambiguous endings, but now I'm stuck in the middle of one.

I don't have time this morning to check in on the horses, but my grandmother swears that they are fine and that I can help with their dinner. She drives me again into town to the deli. "Wouldn't you like a day off?" she asks. "We could get you a manicure and go to the bakery for kolaches."

I must look surprised by the offer. My grandmother is hardly a manicure kind of person.

When I don't say anything, she continues. "You know, the Czech pastries you used to like? The ones with the fruit in the middle. I know you can't eat the sausage ones because they're not kosher."

My eyes must shoot to the window toward Noah, because her voice softens. "I see you have other things on your mind." She pats my hand. "I remember being young, when it feels like you have all the time in the world and not enough. That's how

I felt about your grandfather, too, when we were dating, and again when he got sick, when we were out of time."

My heart aches for her as I have a vague memory of going to see him in the hospital when I was little. "What was he like?" I ask. "I don't remember him that much," I admit.

A smile grows on my grandmother's face that lightens her from within and makes her look decades younger. For the first time, I even see her resemblance to my dad.

"He was very funny, the life of any party. He could talk and talk and make anyone feel comfortable. You know he spent a lot of time here," she says, glancing over at the deli. "He would have loved to see you behind the counter with Abe's grandson. He would have bragged about you for sure. He was very proud of his family."

"Other than my dad," I say, before I see the pained expression on my grandmother's face. "Sorry."

"Your dad and your grandfather butted heads, but that didn't mean your grandfather didn't love him." Her lips tighten into a grim smile, indicating she doesn't want to elaborate.

Uh-oh. I stepped right into that one. Changing the subject, I say, "I didn't know that Grandpa Mel hung out here. I saw pictures of my dad when he worked here, but I didn't know Grandpa Mel spent time here, too."

My grandmother points toward Sol and Irv's booth. "That was his place. Right there. Irv was even a distant cousin of his."

I picture him with his friends before he got sick, and a strange mixture of emotions well up. "Why did Grandpa Mel

and my dad not get along? What was their difference of opin-
ion about?"

My grandmother shakes her head and unlocks the car
doors. "He was mostly disappointed that your dad wanted to
move so far away and didn't visit enough. The rest, well, that's
a story for another day, honey. Go, have fun with Noah. Enjoy
every minute."

Her words are the push I need. I can't necessarily fix the
rift between my parents and my grandmother or right old
wrongs, but I can seize the moment I have with Noah, and I
intend to savor every second we have left.

I scoot past the line of customers, who are looking even
more diverse than the crowd yesterday. There are young college-
student types, families, preppy-looking tourists, and people
of different races and ethnicities and ages. It proves what I
already knew. Jewish food speaks to the soul. The kind of
comfort you can get from a good bowl of matzah ball soup is
universal. Just go to any deli in New York, and it's evident that
the food transcends differences.

I'm thrilled to see it's true here, too. As I enter the store,
Noah's eyes find mine and he gives me a smile that feels like
I'm being enveloped in a rainbow, bright and warm. I'm usually more of a rainy-day person, but that's when I realize that
he brightens everything around me. It's like there's a dimmer
switch and he turns up the dial for me when I enter a room.

Unfortunately, as dazzled as I am by him, the customers
need to be taken care of, so I stop swooning and duck under-
neath the counter and start ringing up once he's planted a kiss

on my forehead. "Hi, you," he says in a deep, quiet voice only I can hear.

"Hi, you, too," I whisper in Noah's direction, in between handing someone a cup of coffee and a bagel.

My next customers are a couple of college students, based on their University of Texas sweatshirts and hats. "So how did you land Bagel Bae?" one of them asks me before turning and snapping a selfie with me, her friend, and Noah, who is waving, out of earshot.

"Landed? Oh, um, I'm not sure that landed is accurate. It's still new and we haven't exactly put a name on it . . . ," I start to say before Noah comes by and puts his arm around my shoulder.

"I'm the lucky one," he says. "I wooed her with my cooking, my Hanukkah gnome, and my Texan charm, right, Hannah?"

I put my finger on my chin like I'm considering. "I think it was the pickles and your hot-dog costume. But yes, consider me fully wooed."

"Aw, you two are way too cute. Can I get a photo?" one of the UT girls asks.

Noah pulls me in even closer and gives me a kiss, right there in the middle of the store as Sol and Irv start to hoot and clap.

"I'm captioning it, hashtag CoupleGoals," the girl says, paying for her food and then leaving.

"I suppose we're social media official," Noah says, pushing

his hair out of his eyes. "I guess I forgot to mention I like public displays of affection. When it comes to you."

I just roll my eyes, but blush. "You like public displays of absolutely everything. Hence the hot-dog costume. We should get back to work." I point to the line forming out the door and try to put on a frown, but I doubt I'm very convincing because my insides are as wiggly as the Jell-O mold dessert my great-grandmother used to make, the one with fruit suspended in it. I, too, am a little stuck.

Noah doesn't mind telling the world how he feels about me. If only he'd tell *me* first for real. I need to know what I mean to him and what the end looks like, before moving forward, if that's what we're doing. The planner in me needs to know so I can plan for the best—and assume the worst, and plan for that, too.

"Wait, what's a Bagel Bae? And why did that girl call me that?" Noah asks.

"Oops. I forgot you're not on social media," I say, pulling out my phone to show him the video. "I can't even stalk you and look at photos of your old girlfriends. It's not fair."

He ignores what I'm saying and just looks at the video in my hand, his eyes widening. When he's watched it three times, he shakes his head and turns away from me for a second. "I honestly don't know whether to kiss you or be mad at you," he says. "Maybe both? I thought they were coming for our food."

"They were! I mean they are." I wince. "But they're coming

for you, too. As am I, Noah," I say, trying to get him to meet my eyes. "I mean, I like pickles an awful lot, so don't get me wrong, but this place has other attractions, too."

He sucks in a breath. "Please cool it on the Bagel Bae stuff. I can't imagine that's what my great-great-great-grandfather Solomon Blum had in mind when he started the place. This deli isn't just about me juggling bagels, okay?"

"What? I bet he'd be excited that his descendent is as hot as his bagels," I say, running a hand on his arm in an attempt to flirt with him, but he gently removes it.

"Sorry." He shrugs. "I know I like to have fun, especially with you, but I take the business seriously. It's important to me, and it's not a joke to anyone but my dad. I need to prove that, and I thought you understood. Why else do you think I roped you into helping me out?"

"Yeah, why else would you want me here?" I ask, taking my hand away and frowning while he gets back to work without further comment, but after some time, he comes by and gives me a quick kiss. "This may have something to do with why I want you here, too." He winks. The tension I felt, imagined or not, dissipates almost instantly.

Once we finally sell out, it's closer to 3:30 today. We have more people coming by to gawk and take photos and fewer people buying lots of food, but it's still steady enough that we're doing really well. We're even selling Blum & Sons T-shirts.

Every once in a while when Noah's not looking, I check my phone to see the image of him kissing me. Hearts float up as more and more people like it, and I imagine it's what my heart would do if it could. The Hannah in this photo is happier and lighter than the one who arrived in Texas still smelling of beer, milkshake, and regret six days ago. I like this version of me much more. The question is whether I can bring her home to New York once she's left Noah behind, because just like falling for him is inevitable, so is leaving him. I'm not sure if I can bear it, but I know I have to, and I have to do it soon. Too soon. Every hour spent in the deli or elsewhere is one fewer one I have here.

Noah also seems a little troubled the rest of the day, which I chalk up to being worried about the deli.

But tonight, we have Hanukkah to celebrate. After we've mopped and cleaned up the tables, we're both a mess again. "I hope one day you'll let me go home and shower first, and maybe put on decent clothes. Unless you find soup stains and horseradish super attractive," I joke as I slide into our booth.

He just grins and leans over to kiss me. "On you? Yes, ma'am. You're beautiful exactly as you are, in your stained shirt with my name on it. Maybe more so."

I throw a Sweet'N Low packet at him. "You're delusional, and a bit of a caveman, but thank you."

He ducks, then holds out two hands, closed. "Pick one."

Hmm. "As I'm left-handed, I'm going to go with the left."

He makes a disappointed face and opens his left hand, which is empty. "Sorry, no Hanukkah surprise tonight."

I pick up a packet of sugar this time, but he laughs and opens his palm. In it is a plain plastic blue dreidel, not even one of the fancy ones from his collection. "I thought we could give it a spin."

"Okay . . . not the most exciting game. Or the best pun." I shrug. "Are you sure there are no puppies involved? Puppies would make dreidel more fun. They could chase them. It would be like the Puppy Bowl, but on Hanukkah."

He tosses the dreidel from hand to hand. "No puppies, but I thought we could make it interesting." He goes over to close the blinds with a wicked smile that makes my heart speed up like a clarinet in a klezmer song, faster and louder by the second.

"How interesting? What did you have in mind?" I manage to squeak out when he sits back down across from me, close enough to touch but not close enough to kiss. In other words, not close enough.

"I want to get to know you better, so I was thinking truth-or-dare dreidel. Is that okay?"

I burst out laughing, but then stop. I'm so risk averse that dares rarely go well for me, and truth, well, I'm not sure how much I'm ready to share, especially about my departure date, which could ruin the little time we have left. But then I glance up at Noah's beautiful brown eyes, which are the color of a good brisket, and just as warm and tender. I trust him. So I nod, then take a swallow of water in front of me.

"I'm in. What are the rules?"

Noah pulls out a piece of paper from his jeans pocket. "Thanks for asking. I know you like to play by the rules, so I came prepared," he says, first getting up and grabbing a pile of coffee beans from a bag on the counter and splitting them between us equally, giving us each about twenty.

When he seems satisfied that we have the same number of beans, he goes back to the paper and begins to read it. "If you land on nun, or none, you get nothing. If you land on shin, you pay one coffee bean in the pot, and if you land on hay, you win half the pot. If you land on gimel, you win the whole pot."

"I know how to pay regular dreidel, Noah. I've been doing it since nursery school. Just ask little David Cohen. I won all his Hanukkah gelt. He may still be mad, now that I think of it. I'm a regular dreidel shark." I laugh. "But where does the truth-or-dare part come in?"

"Good question, Hannah." Noah glances down again at his paper sheepishly. "If you land on nun, you don't do anything. If you land on shin, you have to answer a question. If you land on hay, you get a choice between truth or dare. If you land on gimel, it's dealer's choice. The other person gets to choose truth or dare for you."

I must look nervous because Noah puts his hand over mine. "I don't want you to do anything you don't want to do. Speak up if you feel uncomfortable with anything. Or if it makes you feel better, we can have a safe word, like Moishe Oofnik."

"The grouch from *Shalom Sesame*?" I say with a grin, feeling more at ease already. I wouldn't have remembered that except it was on the other night at his grandfather's place and the Israeli grouch is somehow even more grouchy than his American counterpart.

"Exactly. Just say Moishe Oofnik and we'll stop. No questions asked. Okay? Promise?"

I nod. "I promise."

"Good! Good." Noah pushes his hair out of his face and holds out the dreidel. "You can spin first. If you want."

I grab it from him but before spinning, I look down at my pile of coffee beans. "Why no Hanukkah gelt?"

"A, it tastes terrible, a sorry excuse for chocolate, and B, I couldn't get any in time." He makes an apologetic face. "The only kind at the CVS twenty minutes away had Santa impressions, which defeated the purpose entirely. Who is the target market for that? That's what I want to know."

"I don't know. People who like to be disappointed? It's bad enough we eat matzah. If that's the bread of affliction, maybe Hanukkah gelt is the chocolate of affliction," I say, doing a practice roll with the dreidel. Our dreidel at home is bigger and wooden and has more heft. I'm not used to the small plastic ones, so I spin too hard and it flies completely off the vinyl table.

Noah laughs and goes to pick it up. "Someone's eager," he says, putting it back in my hand. "Easy there."

Biting my lip, I concentrate this time and spin the plastic toy more gently. It goes around and around, tilting and turning as I stare at it, until it finally lands on nun. Nothing. I scowl but hand it back over to Noah.

"Your turn."

"It's just a game, Hannah," he says, his hand lingering on mine.

"No such thing as *just* a game. I play for blood, Mr. Blum," I say, not telling him how my heart is speeding up out of nerves. I don't know what he will ask or dare me to do, and it's disconcerting, to say the least. That's what I don't like about games, the uncertainty, the loss of control. Why should I have my fate dictated by a piece of plastic? I prefer to make my own luck.

Noah rolls his eyes, as his long fingers expertly spin the top, which bounces and then spins in a tight circle.

"Not fair, you've been practicing," I say as the dreidel keeps on going, even picking up speed.

"Maybe a little." He winks as the dreidel lands on shin. He needs to answer a question from me. "Ask away," he says with outstretched arms that he then folds behind his head.

I pretend to think, but I know what I've been dying to ask. "Why did you propose all this?" I gesture to the deli and the dreidel game in front of me.

"Dreidel's a highlight of Hanukkah, Hannah. I thought this one was kind of obvious," he says, tilting his head like he's confused.

"Not just that. I mean why did you offer to spend Hanukkah with me? Was it really just about the deli?" I ask, my voice sounding needy, even to my own ears, so I try to make a joke of it. "Do you do that sort of thing often? I mean do you have a Tu B'Shvat girlfriend that you take tree climbing? Do

145

you have a hot hamantaschen date for Purim who does your dishes?"

Noah leans over the table and plays with a curl in my hair. "I haven't had a girlfriend for a while," he says slowly. "I guess it was a little spur of the moment, but I just had an overwhelming desire to spend time with you and to make you smile, which, by the way, isn't so easy, but it seems to be something at which I excel. More than anything, I wanted to make the holiday special for you. Because you deserve it." He gazes at me, and his usual playful expression is sincere. He's not kidding, and the honesty washes over me like a warm blanket. He may be impulsive, but he has the biggest heart, which he shares with everyone he meets, from the older gentlemen at the deli, to his grandfather, to the people at the senior center, and everyone else lucky enough to know him. Including me. Especially me.

Without saying anything, I lean over myself and kiss him. I can't help it. Words can't express my gratitude. He accepts my kiss, pulling me closer to him and enveloping me with his hands on both sides of my face, until he lets me go all of a sudden with a chuckle in the back of his throat.

"Speaking of cheating. That's no way to win the game. It's your turn to spin."

I spin again, and this time it lands with a thud on shin. I need to answer a question of his.

He looks up at me. "Truth," he says. "I'll give you an easy one. What did you first think when you saw me?"

Noah spreads out his arms as if to show off or something, but he actually looks a little nervous about my answer.

I tilt my head in thought, wondering how much I should reveal. Finally, I decide on letting it all out. "I thought you were the cutest hot dog I'd ever seen, but clearly a little too overconfident. Anyone else would have been mortified to be seen as a wiener. You embraced your wiener hood like you were king of the hot dogs, duke of the deli meat."

He grins. "I'm sorry, I didn't hear anything after 'the cutest dang hot dog I'd ever seen.' . . . If only I had a pickle costume, I *could* have asked you out right then and there. There's no way you would have said no."

"See! Overconfident. I've never once used the word *dang*. Although, now that you mention pickles . . ." I glance pointedly toward the kitchen.

Noah jumps up and bows. "Whatever the lady wishes . . . your weenie is at your command."

"Wiener! And please stop saying that!" I yell toward the kitchen.

He comes back with a dish of pickles a few minutes later and gives me a quick kiss on the cheek before spinning the dreidel. "Don't try to distract me again, Hannah," he says, laughing, but he lands on nun, no moves. "See, you're totally distracting."

"In a good way, right?" I ask, taking back the dreidel. This time I manage the fancy drop-spin move, but it clunks around a couple times before landing on hay. I take half the pot, which isn't much. "I guess I need to choose between truth or dare."

"Feeling daring?" he asks with a twinkle.

I blush but shake my head. Being with Noah, stepping way out of my comfort zone, is more daring than I've been in a while, but it's pretty much my limit. "Not yet. Truth, please."

Noah nods but doesn't push. Instead he leaves his side of the table and slides next to me and looks directly into my eyes, burning with a question. I can tell before he even opens his mouth and whispers in my ear, "Would you rather be somewhere else right now? Tell me honestly."

I think of my parents, Abby, and Becky, and the rest of my friends and everything I'm missing. I can't actually find it in myself to miss much of anything right here in the moment, so I shake my head and whisper back, "No. I want to be right here." As I say it, I know it's the truth, but it's not the whole truth, that I have to leave and I don't know what to do about it.

"With me?" he asks, tracing my jaw with his hand.

I put my hand on the back of his neck and nod. "With you." I lean in farther so I can feel his breath on my cheek. Before I can kiss him, I hold out my other hand and gently drop the dreidel on the table. He gives it a half-hearted spin, not losing eye contact with me.

It lands on gimel.

Dealer's choice. It's up to me.

"Should I dare you?"

"You could, but *gimel* means everything. I already have

everything. All the gimmel I need. Right here, right now," Noah says, pushing his coffee beans to the center of the table. "I'm all in, Hannah."

He may have everything he wants, but in this game of truth or dare, his eyes are daring me to take a chance on him, on us. Unlike dreidel, it's not simple. I can't predict the outcome, but I want to play anyway, because while I could lose big, I could win more time with him.

In fact, in a split second, I envision a future when I come to Texas and visit, he comes to New York to see me, and maybe, just maybe, we go off to the same college and have all the time in the world together with no end in sight. It's a beautiful vision, even if I keep it to myself.

I push my coffee beans into the center of the table as well, where they form a big pile with his. "Me too. I'm all in, too."

12

Night Six of Hanukkah

I'm back in the deli's kitchen early the next morning, but it's more about grabbing extra kisses than preparing extra knishes. Noah's wearing a cowboy hat and twirling me around the kitchen trying to teach me a dance called the Texas two-step, which is part box step, part waltz. I'm flailing and laughing, but eventually I get it and he rewards me with putting his hat on my head.

"Where'd this come from?" I ask. "I haven't seen you wearing it before."

"The hall closet? I think I wanted to be a cowboy for Purim one year." He grins. "I know you said Abby had this idea you'd meet a cowboy and dance with him, so I didn't want to disappoint her." He laughs, then poses for a selfie with me on my phone. "You need to get the full experience."

I'm still flushed, straightening my hair and my apron when the first customers arrive.

Noah's hair is also a mess after putting the hat on himself, but it somehow makes him look even more charming. He winks as he starts up the coffee maker, but surprisingly, I don't need caffeine this morning. Noah is all the boost I need. He's even turned me into a morning person and someone who dances in kitchens with or without music. A Hanukkah miracle for sure.

We're doing our normal routine of scooting past each other to grab bagels and pastries and take-out boxes when I realize how in sync we are. I can anticipate his every move, from the way his long arm stretches, to what he needs based on where he looks or how he smiles. I can see when he gets stressed from the onslaught of customers from the two little lines that pop up between his eyebrows, and I step in to help more when that happens.

We're hanging out behind the counter, not doing much at all between customers. Noah keeps glancing at the door. "Why do you think business is slower today?" he asks before coming behind me and putting his arms around me. "I mean, not that I mind being alone with you and plotting tonight's Hanukkah celebration, but I'm a little concerned we made too much soup."

"I think you are underestimating the amount of soup I can eat. I think I'm one third matzah ball at this point," I say.

His smile is bright, but tight, like he's more worried than he's letting on. Pulling my phone out of my pocket, I look at the TikTok account I started for the deli. It's easier to check it now that he knows about it, although he is tense about the whole Bagel Bae thing, and social media in general. We still have a bunch of followers and some comments, but it's slowing down and other things are popping up. Hanukkah is almost over, and Christmas recipes and decorations are taking over, as they do every year.

But before we lose all momentum, I have one more video to post, the GoFundMe one. I hesitate at first, but glancing over at Noah, I can't bear to see this place he loves close. Not when I can try to do this for them, so I post it, link to the GoFundMe on the bio, then put my phone away, hoping to make a difference. If it works, great. If not, at least I will have tried to help. He can be mad at me later. It's a risk I'm willing to take to help him.

A young couple in jeans and cowboy boots wanders in, and Noah takes off his apron. "Do you mind helping them?" he asks. "I want to finish preparing your Hanukkah surprises."

"No problem!" I tell him, leaning my cheek toward him for a kiss. "I got this. Go work some Hanukkah magic."

Noah flashes me a grateful smile, and I greet the customers, who heard we put tomatillo sauce on our knishes. "Y'all are so inventive," the woman says when I bring her knishes to the table with a side of jalapeños for her husband, who ordered the matzah ball soup.

I chat them up for a few minutes before my phone dings with messages from Abby and Becky. *Can't wait to catch up,* Abby writes. *Lots of DRAMA on ski trip.*

I send a surprised emoji, but I'm not that surprised, really. It's a temple youth group ski trip with other groups from the region. There's always drama with cute guys from school or camp and the other girls in our group of friends. In fact, people go more for the drama than the skiing itself. *Max was there . . . ,* Becky writes, referencing the fleeting crush of mine. *He asked about you like six times.*

Before I left New York, I would have been giddy over this non-news news, even if Becky was prone to exaggeration. He *may* have asked about me once or twice.

Now all the excitement I can manage is a noncommittal thumbs-up, but it's enough for Becky to initiate a three-way FaceTime right away. I duck in the back to not bother the customers and try to swipe my hair out of my face before answering.

"Where are you?" Abby asks before even saying hello.

"The kitchen of the deli, obviously," I say, turning so she can see the commercial-sized fridge, counter, and sink, not to mention the vats of food. "I only have a couple minutes before I have to clear tables and stuff."

"Some vacation," Becky says with a grin. "I bet you miss us."

"It *has* actually been some vacation, but I do miss y'all," I say, but realize that I don't miss them to the same degree as when I arrived a week ago. Maybe it's because I've been so busy, but it's also probably because I've been preoccupied with Noah, who consumes so much of my attention and thoughts.

"Y'all?" Becky laughs. "You are too cute. It must be the fling with Bagel Bae."

I blush but don't answer or correct her about it being more than a fling, because I'm not sure what else I would call it. I also don't correct her that he doesn't want to be called that. If I did, they'd know how I really feel and I'm not ready for that.

A few days here and I'm already talking like a Texan and not as tuned in to what's going on with my friends.

"Hey," Abby says, interrupting. "Did you get your applications in?" Abby is one of the only people in our group of friends as organized and focused as I am. We normally keep each other on track.

It seems like years ago, when all I cared about was which school I was going to go to and where my friends were going to go so we could visit each other. "Yeah, I got them in before I left for Texas. Why?"

"We both got into Binghamton and Penn State already! Yay for rolling admissions. Have you heard?"

"Wow! Congrats! Um, I honestly haven't even looked at my email in days. The Wi-Fi at my grandmother's place is super spotty, and I've been busy."

"Too busy with Noah to start planning your future?" Becky laughs. "We were watching some YouTubes about the dorms to come up with decorating ideas. You're totally going to get in, too, and we can request a triple. That way we don't have to share a bathroom with some random person." Becky wants to be an interior designer, so I just nod as she keeps talking about themes and matching colors and fabric headboards.

Honestly, I don't know if I even want to go to Penn State, or where I want to go. I thought I did, but now I have a Texas-sized ball of uncertainty that's taken up residence in the pit of my stomach.

As if sensing that, Abby interrupts Becky. "Hannah, are you even listening?"

"I think her heart is with the bagel guy," Becky says, but she's not laughing anymore; her eyebrows are furrowed in worry.

I shrug. "What if it's not about him? What if it's about me? I haven't stopped to think about what I really want for years. Maybe I need to figure things out."

My friends look skeptical, but they wish me luck and make me promise to stay in touch.

I should be excited about the future I've been working for since forever, but a few days with Noah and I'm already off that track, which can't happen. If I stick to the plan, I can have everything I want—well, almost everything. Everything but Noah, who I didn't even know I wanted until I met him.

For the first time, I wish we actually hadn't met, that I hadn't seen him in his hot-dog costume or wandered into the deli and agreed to spend Hanukkah together. If we hadn't met, I wouldn't know what I was giving up when I go home. And I maybe would be happier not knowing. I'd be counting down the days until college.

By the time Noah's back, I'm helping other customers at the counter and haven't had a chance to clean up the table. He throws on his apron, gives me a quick kiss with an impish smile, and starts cleaning up for me. For a moment, I just watch. It's silly, but I try to memorize how he hums to himself, how he almost dances while walking between the tables and sweeping, like he's in a boy band.

After we've been cleaned out of rugalach and a batch of new customers buying pastry for their bridge club has left, I catch Noah frowning at the empty dishes.

I walk over to where he's standing and throw my arms around his waist. "I missed you," I say, but he tenses up for a second before relaxing.

"Yeah?" he asks, turning around to face me. "How much?"

I look up at his face. Again, he seems a little worried about something. Not wanting to pry, I answer honestly. "Too much."

Noah's eyebrows knit together. "Why were there jalapeños and tomatillo sauce on the table?"

I grab a couple of the dishes and shrug. "I told them it was a special, and they went for it! I put it on TikTok, too."

I answer him with a big smile, but it fades off my face quickly when I see his reaction.

He rubs his face with his hand. "Hannah, I appreciate what you're trying to do, but this is my family's deli. Please don't change the menu without asking, or post beefcake bagel boy pictures. Okay? I have everything under control. I can do this. I have to do this my way." His voice is strained like he's trying not to be upset but really is annoyed at me. "Please?" he asks more gently.

"Okay, whatever you want. I'm sorry. I was just trying to help. But change can be good; maybe it's time to refresh the menu and come up with some new ideas. Attract new customers!"

"Just let me handle it," he says, more firmly than I've heard him before, so I nod.

A second later, his face brightens and he reaches out for my hand. "Wait until you see what I have planned for tonight. . . . It's a good one, but we have to drive for about an hour. Oh, and dress warm."

I smile at him but realize that it's our second-to-last night together and I haven't told him yet. Tonight is going to have to be the time I tell him, as much as I would love to put it off again. If I put it off any longer, it will be that much worse.

My grandmother picks me up on time so that Noah can have more time to close the deli and get ready to pick me up in an hour. She takes one look at his upbeat smile and, as soon as we're in the car, studies my face. "You haven't told him, have you?"

I wince. "That obvious?"

"You don't think you owe him the truth? I've known that boy since he was little, and while he sure smiles a lot, he's like my old yellow lab, sweet but skittish. He needs everyone to love him but has problems trusting. You don't want to make that worse, do you?"

"Nana, are we still talking about Noah or your dog?"

My grandmother lets out a sigh. "Both? You know, Hannah, if something's meant to be, it has a way of working out."

I shake my head. "I don't believe in bashert, or soulmates, or anything like that. I believe in plans and I have one that's back in New York. I can't afford distractions. Okay, maybe I can for a few more days, but that's it." Thinking of my conversation with Abby and Becky, I realize that Noah's not the only one counting on me. "I need to look at colleges, pick one, and focus on my future."

"Plans change," Nana says, but purses her lips and doesn't say anything more.

An hour later, Noah is actually on time. I'm ready, too, and dressed in the warmest clothes I brought with me, a heavy sweatshirt, gloves and hat that were in the bottom of my suitcase, and jeans. It's overkill for Texas. I can't imagine we could drive anywhere in an hour cold enough to warrant this, but I humor him when he hands me a hot cup of cocoa. "I didn't know if you liked whipped cream or marshmallows, so I did both," he says. "And a dash of chili powder for spice to keep you warm."

I sip the drink in the truck once I blow on it to cool it down. "Thanks," I say, not mentioning that earlier today he was annoyed at me for serving spicy sauce and peppers at the deli and now he's spicing up the hot chocolate because it was his idea.

Noah connects his phone to the car. "Some music to get us in the mood for tonight," he says with a grin. I'm not sure what to expect, something romantic? Six versions of "I Have a Little Dreidel"? It's not like there's *that* much Hanukkah music out there.

But it seems Noah rose to the challenge, starting his play list with Adam Sandler's updated Hanukkah song, then going into Daveed Diggs's "Puppy for Hanukkah," and then Idina Menzel from *Frozen* singing "Ocho Kandelikas," a jazzy Hanukkah song in Ladino, which is a Jewish Spanish language.

"Solid playlist," I say. "But I doubt you can keep it up for a full hour."

"I did have to get creative," Noah says, skipping over a klezmer version of "Oh Hanukkah," for "Let It Snow."

"Um, technically, this isn't a Hanukkah song at all. No dreidels or menorahs or Maccabees involved." I raise an eyebrow but hum along because the song is absolutely a bop, as far as holiday songs go.

"Ah, this is what I mean by creative, Hannah. We've now transitioned into winter songs written by Jewish composers, which should be a Jeopardy category all on its own. As you can imagine, there wasn't as much of a market in the 1930s, forties, and fifties for openly Jewish songs, so the composers paid the bills and made names for themselves by writing things like 'White Christmas,' 'Rudolf,' and 'Silver Bells.' I always thought it was wild that Jews invented the whole idea of a white Christmas. Probably Jews in New York City and California who didn't have to shovel snow."

"Huh. So you're saying we could have had better Hanukkah songs if Jewish composers weren't writing Christmas songs," I joke, but Noah's serious.

"No, I'm actually saying that Jewish history and assimilation are kinda complicated."

"I never really thought of it that way," I say.

"That's because you live in New York and don't have to assimilate as much. Jewish culture and New York culture vibe pretty well," Noah says, glancing over at me for a second before focusing on the road again as "Rockin' Around the Christmas Tree" comes on.

"But maybe they just enjoyed spreading joy through their music and looked at it as writing American music rather than religious music. A lot of the composers were immigrants who were happy to be in America considering what was going on in Europe."

I think of my grandmother and how she didn't correct the woman in the general store who wished me a merry Christmas. While I still disagree about keeping quiet, it's true that being Jewish in New York City is very different from being Jewish in rural Texas or most other places.

"I think you'd like my dad," I say. "He loves talking about history. He'd probably try to convince you to major in it," I say, but Noah shakes his head.

"I prefer to learn history from the people who lived it, and from the History Channel, than books, but that's just me. There are more aliens building pyramids on the History Channel than in textbooks. . . ."

I laugh, but as I do, I realize he dodged talking about his own plans for college, maybe on purpose because he keeps saying he's not a planner like me, but then I think of what my grandmother said about him. Maybe Noah's skittish about it.

"But what about college?" I press a little.

Noah frowns, looking straight ahead at the road. "I don't know. I may take a gap year to work at the deli full-time. I may do community college part-time. My dad doesn't like either option. So we'll see."

He tries to smile, but by the way his jaw tenses, I know I shouldn't press any further. It's clearly a source of tension, but it concerns me that he's so unclear about his future because what does it mean for us if he doesn't have his own act together? How can he fit into mine?

"Whenever I want my parents to change their mind about something, I create a slide presentation with research, facts, and different kinds of charts. I find it can be very persuasive," I say.

Noah laughs. "That story doesn't surprise me in the least."

I swat at him. "How do you think I got a phone in sixth grade? Or a rabbit in fourth grade?"

"Okay, I'll keep the Hannah method in mind for future needs." He smiles.

I'm lost in thought for a while, but after about five more Jewish-written holiday songs, we're at our location near the campus of Texas A&M, one of the biggest colleges in the state.

"An ice rink?" I ask with a smile. "Wait, do you know how to skate?"

"Not exactly," Noah admits. "But I figure you do. Your

grandmother said you go skating every year in Central Park, or some other park, and I thought you would like this while you're here. There's a skating rink in a mall in Houston, but I assumed that would be less your thing because of commercialization and all that."

"I do love to skate," I confirm. "Although part of the fun is being outdoors under the stars, but in this case, I'll allow for indoor skating. Not in a mall. That's just weird and wrong."

He looks relieved as he grabs his own gloves from the back seat, along with a hat and knee pads and elbow pads.

"Was this part of your preparation for tonight?" I giggle.

"It was mostly making the playlist and hot chocolate. The padding is left over from when I thought I could teach myself to skateboard. Spoiler, it's way harder than it looks and the ground is hard. But who needs all your ribs?"

I wince but follow him into the rink, where he pays for our tickets and skate rentals before I can offer. The rink is twice as big as the ones I'm used to and is full of families, teenagers, and twentysomethings skating around to pop music. Some of the skaters are slow and clinging on to the wall and some are fast, dashing in between other skaters, spinning, jumping, and skating backward. I'm a fairly decent skater. Although I've never taken lessons, I can skate backward, on one leg, and manage a small spin. It won't get me into the Olympics, but it's probably enough to impress a Texan who can't skate at all.

Once our skates are on and we start to make our way to the entrance to the rink, I notice Noah is fairly wobbly, so I

kneel down and tighten his skates. "I should be embarrassed."
He grins. "But if it means I don't fall, that's probably less embarrassing, right?" he says as I hold out my hand to him.

"Have I mentioned I don't usually do this?" he asks, flash-
ing me a grateful grin as I step out onto the smooth ice and
wait for him to follow. He holds on tight and takes small steps
like he's walking in boots. Feeling him wobble back, I hold on
tight and pull him up.

"You can do this." I squeeze his hand and look him in
the eyes.

"Thanks," he says, looking longingly at the wall once I've
led him away from it. His nose is already adorably red from
the cold, and his eyes are concentrating on his feet in front
of him.

"It helps if you don't look down," I say, gently pushing a
couple times with my feet so we glide forward. "Just concentrate on balancing and look in front of you. Hold out your
other arm for balance."

He nods but holds on even tighter to my hand as we
slowly make our way around the rink. "I don't think I'm a
cold-weather-sports person," he says, "but I'm good in the sun.
You'll have to come back when we can go tubing down the
river. That's more my speed, to be honest. There's a reason
why they call it a lazy river. Also, it doesn't involve putting
tiny blades on your shoes and hoping for the best."

"I'd like that," I say, turning so I'm skating backward and
looking at his eyes. He glances down once, but when I squeeze

his hands, he looks back up at me and his eyes light up. At first I think it's something I said until the music comes over the loudspeaker along with a voice from an announcer.

"And now, in honor of Hanukkah, give a big howdy to Hillel of Texas A&M, the loudest and proudest in the nation, as they present this special ice show."

"Hava Nagila" starts playing, and soon a bunch of college-aged people are skating in a circle around the ice in a circle and the rest of the skaters stop to watch.

"Is this a Hanukkah flash mob?" I laugh. "On ice? Oh, Noah, I think you've outdone yourself. This I didn't see coming. It's like Disney on Ice but with Jews instead of Mickey Mouse. I love it."

I laugh even harder as a guy dressed as a giant, fluffy blue dreidel makes his way onto the ice and waves at us. Noah gingerly extracts a hand from me and waves to him before grabbing on to the side of the rink for balance.

"Someone you know? Forget I asked. *Of course* you would know the only guy at Texas A&M dressed as a dreidel. You probably even hooked him up with the costume."

Noah gives me a sheepish shrug. "That's Eli. He's Sol's grandson. He's president of the Hillel chapter and may have helped arrange it. Maybe."

"I didn't even think they'd have Hillel here."

Noah raises an eyebrow, or maybe it's frozen that way. "It was one of the first ones in the entire country, actually. I think it's over a hundred years old."

"Huh. Who knew. You should totally apply here. Just

think, next year it could be you in the dreidel costume. I mean, if you learn how to skate. It looks heavy." I smile before I remember that college is a sore spot, but he just shrugs.

"Yeah, in Texas we get automatic acceptance if you're in the top ten percent of your class, so I can go here, or almost any state school. UT is six percent. If I decide to go. We'll see. I don't want to leave my grandfather or the deli."

He looks so uninterested in the subject, or maybe conflicted, that I don't know what to say. "Um, that's amazing. I wish we had that."

He puts an arm around me and focuses back on the show, so I do the same. The skaters start pairing off and twirling each other, then go back in the circle and form an intricate pattern, one hand over another, weaving in and out of the circle like some sort of elaborate maypole dance. "Wow," I say. "This is kinda awesome. How do they not bump into each other?"

Eventually, the song is over, the students bow, and I'm clapping fiercely but quietly due to my heavy gloves muffling the noise. The performance was not serious and quiet, like I thought I wanted, but somehow celebrating Hanukkah this way did bring me more joy than I thought possible. The students were doing far more than skating. They were celebrating openly, saying we're here and we're proud. We can be Texan and Jewish, which apparently they had been doing for more than a hundred years, albeit maybe not in ice skates.

After Noah fist-bumps with the dreidel, thanks him, and introduces me, we're both ready for hot chocolate, and I'm ready to finally tell him what I've been dreading. But it's slow going making my way around the ice with him. Five-year-olds and middle school kids skate past us quickly. "Show-offs!" I mumble.

Noah is still smiling, seemingly proud of the surprise. "Wait until you see what I have planned for tomorrow night. Lucky number seven . . . You have bail money and life insurance, right? How about a parachute?"

I must look at him funny because he stops skating and takes my face in his cold gloves. "I'm kidding. I would never let anything hurt you. No need for insurance."

I swallow, and the cold air burns my lungs. "I know. I'm not worried about that. But there's something I need to tell you." I pause but then suck in another icy breath. "I have to leave tomorrow. I won't be here for the rest of Hanukkah."

I could almost see it happening, the doors of his heart closing on me, locking me out. Skittish like Nana's dog. He would run away if he could, before I run first. "When were you going to tell me, Hannah?"

I shake my head. "I just found out yesterday. My parents were able to get me a flight out, and the only one they could get is on Christmas Eve. It will just be me, a bunch of other Jews, and some reindeer," I try to joke, but it falls completely flat.

"And you weren't going to tell me until right before you left?" His face falls. "Instead, you just let me go on thinking we had more time," he says, leaning over on the railing.

"I didn't want to ruin everything. You knew I had to leave

at some point to go back to New York. I have to go home. Blum where you're planted, right? I'm planted in New York."

I open my mouth to say something, anything that would make it better, when all of a sudden a kid in hockey skates executes a fast, hard stop near me, and before I can get out of the way, ice and snow fly all over me. I must look ridiculous. I thought I was at my lowest point in the airport, but now I know that's not the case because I didn't really care what the people at the airport thought of me. I do care about Noah and his thoughts. One look at his face and I know I've hurt him, more than he's letting on because I don't know what's colder, the ice in my hair and eyelashes or the expression on Noah's face.

I brush myself off, shivering. We walk to the exit of the rink separately, no more hot chocolate or playlists mentioned even after we take off our skates and return them and make our way to the truck for a long ride home. I'm sore, but it's more than my butt, or my feelings. It's my heart this time, and I'm not sure how it will recover.

13

We barely talk the whole ride home. It's clear he's hurt, just as it's equally clear that I don't know how to fix things, or if I should even try to get past his shields. Maybe it's kinder to let him go.

To break the tension, I put the radio on the first crappy, non-holiday music channel I can find. I'm just not feeling the holiday spirit right now, not after tonight. The channel is playing eighties music and not even the decent kind my mom likes. It's the really cheesy, one-hit-wonder kind, and yet, it's better than silence, small talk, or hard conversations.

When we pull onto my grandmother's gravel road, Noah's face is serene but devoid of human emotion, not unlike the polite, disinterested mask I put on in New York. Robot Noah is far less appealing than goofy hot dog Noah, or romantic cowboy Noah, or confident cooking-show Noah. The mask is the kind no one can penetrate, the one that makes me unable to be hurt, although I have a feeling he is as devastated as I am, only he's not showing it outwardly.

His voice cracks as he pulls off his hat and smooths down his hair. "I hope you have a safe flight. If you give me your address in New York, I can send you a check for your work this week."

"That's not necessary," I say, my eyes pleading with his. "I didn't do this for the money. I did it for you, and your grandfather."

"I know," he practically whispers, giving me a brief kiss on the forehead and raising his voice. "Happy Hanukkah, Hannah Levin, who is just visiting. I'll try to come by tomorrow and say goodbye. It was nice knowing you," he says, and maybe it's my imagination, but I think he wipes away a tear when his back is turned.

I take a few steps toward the porch, where I can see my grandmother peeking out before replacing the curtain, probably to give us some privacy. By the time I turn around to say something else, he's started the truck and is backing up toward the road.

This wasn't how I wanted to say goodbye, especially after last night, and the last several days, but as sunny and bright as Noah is when he's happy, this is like his normal personality has been eclipsed by a dark cloud. And I'm the dark cloud.

My grandmother opens the door and meets me with some hot cocoa. "You look like you can use this. I assume it didn't go well."

I drop all my winter clothes in a pile and sink down on the couch with the hot cocoa, letting it warm my cold hands.

"Do you want to talk about it?" Nana asks after a few minutes of silence.

I look over at her and put my drink on the coffee table, then throw my head back on the couch. "I guess you were right. I should have told him earlier. And I should have spent more time with you. I'm sorry. I just got swept away."

She pats my hand and pulls me into a hug. After she lets go, she pulls herself off the couch. "I have something for you," she says as she walks toward a cabinet in the dining area.

Once there, she pulls out a plain cardboard box and brings it gingerly to where I am, placing it on the table. "Go ahead and open it."

The brown box is falling apart from age. It's soft on one side from possible water damage, and ripped on another side, yet considering the anticipation on her face, I open it, unsure what I'm going to find.

Inside is a slightly tarnished silver menorah without any special embellishments or decorations. It's heavy in my hands, like it may be made of real silver or pewter or some other precious metal, but age has ravished its once-beautiful appearance.

Not waiting for a reaction, my grandmother leans over to help me unwrap it from the pink tissue paper, which is falling apart as I touch it. "This was your grandfather's and his father's before him. I didn't know where it was. I haven't seen it since he got sick, but I managed to dig it out today. I'm sure he would have wanted you to have it, especially considering how you've been trying to rekindle the flame of Jewish life here in Rosenblum."

"The flame," I say carefully, holding the menorah in my hand, which isn't the prettiest I've ever seen, certainly not as pretty as the artisan-made one my mom bought at the Jewish Museum in the city, but maybe the most meaningful in my family. "Like the ner tamid, the eternal flame. It's supposed to be always lit, no matter what. Like the Jewish presence in this town. Someone needs to be keeper of the flame."

Turning it over in my hand, I start to understand what Noah was trying to tell me about this place. I kept urging him to leave, telling him that he doesn't need to take on the burden of representing the entire Jewish history of Rosenblum all by himself, but what if he feels like he has to be the keeper of the flame? And I completely ignored and assumed that he needed to move away to be successful, to fit into my ideas and his dad's.

I didn't see him or listen, and that was probably a big part of how I hurt him.

"Thanks, Nana," I say, hugging her, my throat dry with emotion. "I will treasure it."

She sits back on the couch, seemingly satisfied.

"Why didn't you give this to my dad when Grandpa Mel died?" I ask.

She shrugs. "I couldn't bear going through his things at first, and your dad had issues with how your grandfather expressed, or didn't express himself as a Jew."

The menorah in my hand, not to mention the various

other signs of Jewish life in the house like shabbat candles and the kiddush cup in the cabinet look pretty Jewish to me.

"I don't get it."

She pats my hand, her eyes sparkling with tears. "I know you don't. Not yet. I want to tell you something important. It's about your dad and grandfather."

I stand up to get her a tissue, which she accepts with a small nod. "I tried not to take sides. I loved my husband, and I love my son. Your grandfather believed that the best thing for our family was to be quietly Jewish in the home, but to fully integrate into the community, to eat where and what our neighbors eat, to fit in as much as possible, so that no one would think any less of us or treat us any differently. He thought it would be easier. We had a mezuzah, but it was inside the door, not outside. We lit the menorah, but we didn't put it in the window. Your grandfather had his reasons, his fears," she says, dabbing at her eyes.

"But when your dad went off to college, he started exploring that side of him. He joined Hillel; he met your mom and her family. He didn't want to be quietly Jewish anymore. He wanted to be part of a more vibrant community; to do this, he felt he had to move away, which broke your grandfather's heart. Before he left, they had a big fight and your dad called your grandfather a coward."

My grandmother's hands are clutching at the tissue, an outward sign of her deep distress at telling the story of the painful rift, even if it was two decades ago. "They made up, of course, when your grandfather got sick, but things were never the same, and I don't think he forgave me either."

"What did you do, Nana? It sounds like it was really between them, and they were both grown men. Stubborn ones, too."

My grandmother shakes her head. "I didn't do enough to make peace, to tell your dad when your grandfather first was diagnosed and didn't want me to tell anyone. I feel awful about all the years we lost. Even after your grandfather died." She waves her hand as if to dismiss the last comment. "You're here now," she says. "And you're old enough that you should know and make your own decision about how to lead your life, what kind of person, and Jew you want to be. But the other reason I'm telling you this, Hannah, is that you should never wait to apologize to someone you've hurt. Time is too precious."

With this she stands, pats my knee one more time, and slowly walks over toward her bedroom. "Good night, Hannah darlin'. I love you."

"I love you, too, Nana," I say as she nods once and closes the door to her bedroom.

Looking at the closed door, I realize I may have massively messed up things with Noah, but I did something I didn't think possible a week ago. I developed my own, deep bond with my grandmother, and despite everything else that happened over the week, I can't regret coming here for that alone.

I also know I need to heed her words. I said I was sorry to

Noah tonight, but not really. I didn't truly apologize with my heart, the way my rabbi encourages us to apologize to those we've wronged every year before Yom Kippur. Noah deserves more than my non-apology apology, so I have to make sure I tell him tomorrow before it's too late. It's not something that can wait until another day or another holiday.

14

Night Seven of Hanukkah

Seven no longer feels like a lucky number to me, not when I wake up to pack. My flight isn't until the late afternoon, but I'm hoping Noah stops by earlier like he said. I pace the floor after breakfast, but no Noah.

My grandmother shoots me a sympathetic look over her coffee. "Why don't you go check in on the horses and say goodbye to them? I'll send Noah out there if he comes."

"Good idea," I say, grabbing my coat and phone and putting on my boots. At the barn, the horses prick up their ears when I arrive. Ringo nuzzles me when I hand him a carrot. Paul is even more excited, swishing his tail and sighing when I rub his nose. "Yeah, I'm going to miss you, too, guys." My eyes water, which is probably a combination of forgetting to take my antihistamine and sincere sadness about not seeing the horses again. "You guys helped me get through a tough week," I mumble. "I won't forget it."

At that point, Elvis walks in, eager for attention, wagging his tail and barking at me and the horses. I hand him a couple biscuits from a shelf and head out of the barn, overcome with emotion.

When I get back in the house, I glance at the rooster clock in the kitchen. It's nine a.m. My stomach drops, heavy from the oatmeal sitting in it, but more so by the realization that if Noah was going to come over before work, he would have already been here. The fact that he didn't bother to stop by means he's closed the door on us.

Sensing my disappointment, my grandmother takes her car keys out of her pocket. "I can drive you over there if you want to talk to him," she says.

I push my hair out of my face and close my eyes to think. While I should probably let him move on, I know I can't leave without trying to talk to him one more time, at least to apologize. Maybe it's a little selfish, but I need him to know what this week has meant to me, what *he* has meant to me, and that I'm truly, deeply sorry for last night.

"Nana," I manage to choke out. "I'd really like a ride over there."

She heads to the front door without another word, and I follow. While it took some getting used to, I now understand that my grandmother is good about allowing silence when it's needed, something that I especially appreciate right now since I need to figure out exactly what to say.

Unfortunately, by the time my nana pulls into the town square, none of the words swimming around in my head are even close to capturing how I'm feeling, part nauseated, part hopeful, and fully regretful. For the first time, I think I need to tackle something so big without a plan, and I'm scared of what will happen, but more scared if I don't do anything.

When I get close to the deli, I see a line leading up to the door, which isn't super surprising, but what is perplexing is that the closed sign is still on the door.

"I wonder what's going on," I say to my grandmother. "I better go check it out."

"Okay, honey," Nana says. "I'm going to go to the general store. Call me if you need me."

I mutter my thanks, but my mind is already somewhere else, close to panicking. Noah may be impulsive, but it's not like him to just close the deli for no reason. He loves this place and is trying to save it. Closing without a sign on the door explaining why isn't a good move, which he would know.

I excuse myself as I push through the line and peek in the window, but the blinds are down. I can't see anything. What if I hurt him even more than I thought and he's in a ball crying? Or he's been hit by a car? I pick up my phone and text him. He may not want to talk to me, but he could at least confirm he's okay.

Hey, I'm outside the deli, which is closed. You okay?

I wait a minute, two minutes, even five minutes, fully pacing. The line of customers behind me is growing. Then I pick up the phone and call, but it goes straight to voice mail. I hang up, then call right back. Same thing. Now I'm completely worried. Where could he be that his phone isn't on?

I call back again and leave a message. "Noah, it's Hannah. You're not answering, and the deli is closed. I'm getting seriously concerned." I walk briskly to the back of the deli and knock on the door, hard, but no one answers.

That's when I call my grandmother, who's still in line at the general store. "Nana, I need to help out here. I'm so sorry."

The other end of the line is quiet at first. "Let me run a few things home, and then I'll swing back to help you," she says.

I thank her, and at the same time, I dig around my bag and find my key to the deli. I was planning on returning it to Noah, but I'm glad I still have it.

Smiling at the customers, I walk over to the door and let myself in. "Just give me five minutes," I tell them.

Once inside, I turn on the lights. Everything looks more or less normal. Dishes in the kitchen are done. Tables are clean. Whatever happened, it was very recent. As I'm debating opening the deli by myself, the restaurant's phone rings. Hoping it's Noah, I pick it up on the first ring.

"Hello?" I ask, breathless from lunging for the phone.

"Hi, who's this?" a motherly voice asks.

"Oh, sorry. This is Hannah. How can I help you? I mean,

if you're trying to call Blum and Sons. The deli is kinda closed right now, but I'll pass on the message."

"Oh, Miss Hannah. This is Consuela. Mr. Abe told me all about you. I was just calling to check in on him. Is Noah there?"

"Hi, it's nice to meet you. Noah's told me about you and your husband, too. Have you talked to Noah or Abe? I haven't been able to reach Noah, and it's unlike them not to open the store."

"Oh, honey. I talked to them last night. Abe's got pneumonia. Noah's probably taking care of his grandfather. But things must not be good if he isn't at work. He was planning on opening today."

I peek out the blinds, and the line is still there. "Consuela, I mean, Miss Consuela, could you talk me through opening on my own? I don't want to let all of their customers down." I may not be able to stay, but this at least I could do. When we started, I promised Noah I'd help save the business, so now's as good a time as any to keep that promise.

"Sure, Hannah," she says. "That's mighty kind of you to do that for them. I'm sure Mr. Abe will appreciate it when he's well. Here's what you do. . . ."

I scribble down all of her directions on what I can grab from the fridge and freezer, where everything is, and when deliveries will be made. I get the recipe for matzah balls over the phone, too. Ten minutes later, I've got my apron on and the door is open.

"Hi, welcome to Blum and Sons. What can I get y'all?" I say, unpacking some bagels that were apparently made fresh yesterday. Luckily, they still feel soft enough to sell, although it may not be ideal.

The coffee is brewing, but the customers are fine waiting at the counter and chatting with one another. The next hour or two go by in a blur, so much so that I don't get a chance to look at my phone until the morning rush is over.

"Sorry, Nana!" I say when she enters the store. I smile at the customer in front of me and give my grandmother a one-minute sign with my finger. "Apparently Abe has pneumonia, so I'm filling in to help out."

My grandmother hesitates before saying, "You know we need to leave for the airport in two hours."

I hand over the coffee to the woman in line, then a paper bag with her bagel and cream cheese. "Thank you so much! Please come back, ma'am," I say when she leaves a dollar tip on the counter for me.

Before someone else approaches, I grab an extra apron and hand it to my grandmother, who raises an eyebrow but puts it on with a grin as she comes behind the counter with me and washes her hands. "I know we don't have much time, Nana. I'll give it another hour, and if I can't reach Noah, I guess I'll have to leave for the airport," I say, glancing at my phone again. There's still no message from him. Just a text from Consuela checking in to see how I'm doing and another couple of texts from Abby and Becky about our plans once I return.

"Okay, sweetie, put me to work."

I give her a quick hug, which she returns. A grateful tear threatens to form in my eye, but she stands up tall and smooths her apron.

"I'm happy to help," she says. "I just want to spend the time that we have left together."

Of course, my grandmother is a natural, even if she can't figure out how to use the register. She greets most people by name, handing over their food with a smile and a lot of personal small talk.

Soon it's eleven o'clock, and I'm being slammed again by customers. "Hey, you're the bagel babe!" one of them says, pointing at a T-shirt she's wearing that looks like something she printed herself. *Bagel Babe Seeking Bagel Bae,* it says, with a picture of two bagels in cowboy hats holding hands. They weirdly resemble me and Noah if we were actually food, not people.

My eyes must be popping out of my head in shock as my grandmother chuckles and I glare at her. "Um, where did you get that from?"

She laughs. "Our Hillel printed them for our bake sale. Cute, right? The proceeds went to tzedakah."

"Sure," I say, wondering if maybe the TikTok thing went a little too far after all, although tzedakah, i.e., charity, which is translated literally as justice, is always a good thing.

"Where is the Bagel Bae?" she asks, looking around.

By this time, a small crowd has gathered and I'm making sandwiches, ringing up coffee, and handing over change all at once. "Good question," I tell her. "I think there's some sort of family emergency." I frown, looking at the wall clock. It's eleven-thirty at this point, and I don't know how long I can keep this up between my pending flight and running out of food. We have about a dozen bagels left, if that, enough rye bread and challah and salads to hopefully get us through the lunch shift. Even the pickles are running low, as is my hope that I can see Noah and explain before I need to leave.

I keep going for now, despite the sweat forming on my neck, my tired feet, sore from wearing the wrong shoes to work, and my dashed hopes. At least I can leave Noah and his grandfather with happy customers and a full cash register, if nothing else. When it seems like things are quiet for the moment, I leave Nana at the counter and run to the bathroom and splash some water on my face. When I come back, I put my purse on the shelf behind the register; as I do, a pile of mail falls on the floor. I lean down to pick it up and immediately notice the first letter on top of the pile.

It's a thick one, from Cornell addressed to Noah, and it's already opened. A thick letter at college admissions time can only mean one thing. He's been accepted, either early decision or early action. Either way, it means they really, really want him. The other thing: the open envelope means that he knows he's been accepted to a school not that far from me and he's chosen not to tell me. And he's blaming me for leaving when it's in his power to come to New York and he's not even thinking about the option.

Blum where you're planted. That's his motto, and he's planted in Rosenblum, Texas, for good.

I had come here to apologize for leaving, but he'd shut the door on me already, way before I left. But then I turn over the envelope and see the postmark. It's from yesterday. He may have just gotten the news after finding out I was leaving, or right before I told him my new departure date. I start scrubbing the counter where a customer dripped coffee, furiously trying to figure out what I think it means and what I hope it means. Could there still be a chance for us?

It's hard to know when I can't even reach him. I want to run upstairs and knock on the door again, but the clock is ticking, literally, the customers piling in, and my heart is running a 5K trying to keep up with everything going on in front of me, and inside me. To make matters worse, my grandmother is taking off her apron and putting her purse on her shoulder, a reminder that it's time to go, but I decide then and there. I'm not leaving town. Not yet. I have to see this through.

15

My grandmother takes the news in stride. Somehow,
I think she's not all that surprised, especially after the pep talk
she gave me. She promises to talk with my folks and rearrange
my flight. I don't know how they are going to react, but I honestly don't have time to worry about that. I have more Jewish
food to serve before we close early for Christmas Eve in two
hours. It's not even my deli, but I feel responsible for making
sure everyone has what they need for the holiday, a little bit
of Jewish soul sent home with them in a paper bag with the
Blum logo on it.

The customers later on in the day are a combination of
people picking up items for breakfast for Christmas Day and
Jews from farther away stocking up. Everyone is in a rush, but
they generally leave satisfied. It helps that Consuela has given

my grandmother instructions and shopping lists so she can help me throughout the day, until we're finally ready to close.

Once I've smiled at the last customer and sent my grandmother home to feed the horses, I can start cleaning up and pondering what I've done by missing my flight, my promise to celebrate Hanukkah with my friends and my family. A week ago, I would have stuck to my plan no matter what. As I wipe down the counters and clear the dirty dishes, I realize that it's not just my plans that have changed over the past week. It's me.

Only seven days ago, I couldn't have pictured myself cleaning stalls, caring about horses, working my butt off at someone's store when I could be bingeing shows and texting all day with my friends. I also couldn't imagine that I'd find a ridiculous boy, decide he's not ridiculous after all, fall in love with him, only to lose him.

But here I am, mop in hand and no boy in sight. When I finish cleaning up and the place looks better than when I arrived, I have one more thing to do. I head to the kitchen, phone in hand with the recipe Consuela has sent me.

I've eaten matzah ball soup most of my life. It doesn't seem that difficult to make, until I actually try to do it myself. No wonder Zabar's charges so much. This recipe is no joke.

I read it over and can't do any of the first few steps, as I don't have an actual way of making quick chicken broth by hand. Yet, if I want to have this done in a few hours, I'm going to have to take shortcuts. I run over to the pantry in search of cans of chicken broth. Nope, nothing. Of course, Abe would make his own probably with a recipe that has been passed on for a hundred years and only exists in his head. I dig through the freezer but don't see any broth or bones there either.

I'm contemplating asking Consuela for advice again, when my phone buzzes with incoming texts from Josh, Becky, and Abby.

More snow???? Are you ever coming home?

We should have applied to Tulane. I haaaaaaate this weather.

I hope we see you by Valentine's Day.

I didn't apply to Tulane . . . but I did apply to two Texas schools, which I had mentioned to my friends, but we all laughed about it at the time. It doesn't seem so funny now that I've grown attached to the place, and more importantly, some of the people here. Especially one person, and that scares me more than I want to admit.

I look at the news on my phone and see there's more chaos at the airport. It's like someone's telling me I made the right call to stay. It's almost like it's fated. Bashert. That I be here at this moment, cooking this soup with love, but not with chicken stock because apparently there isn't any and all the stores are now closed.

The last thing I want to do is to bother Consuela on Christmas Eve. From what Noah tells me, she doesn't get to see her family that often. She deserves a break, and I need to figure this out for myself.

Then it hits me. Veggie stock. I can make stock out of

vegetables. It won't have that chicken flavor, but it should still be healthy and help Abe and Noah feel better. Now that the deli's closed, there's nothing else I can do, so I get started cooking the vegetables. I sauté garlic, onion, some celery, and carrots with olive oil for about ten minutes before I add a bunch of other scraps of vegetables I find around the kitchen including peppers, basil, parsley, tomatoes, spinach, potatoes, and whatever else I can find, pouring water over it with a pinch of salt to simmer. It doesn't look like much right now, but I hope it has the potential to become something special. Just like I think—no, I know that Noah and I have that potential, if only he will see it, too.

I turn up the heat, as the recipe on my phone says, and wait for it to boil. Of course, it doesn't do so right away, and I can't force it to do what I want, no matter how hard I stare at it or how high I turn up the heat, so I bring my attention to the matzah ball portion of the recipe.

I mix the egg, the matzah meal, veggie oil, salt, and pepper until it looks disgusting. It's a wonder that anything so gross can be so delicious, but if there's anything I've learned it's that I jump to too many conclusions and need to trust more, so I stick the mixture in the fridge for a while until my broth is boiling and I turn it down to simmer.

Now that I have downtime, I finally have the chance to call my mom. She answers on the first ring. "How are you, sweetie?" she asks gently, more gently than usual, which probably means my grandmother has filled her in on Noah's disappearing act and my feeble attempt to make everything better one matzah ball at a time.

"Let's just say I'm not getting a summer job at Zabar's. I'll leave it at that."

"You know, Hannah, it's okay to screw up and make mistakes. It's also okay not to know what you're doing. I'm sorry if I ever gave you the impression that you needed to be perfect and have everything figured out. You should fail spectacularly and learn from it. Also, I'm impressed. Missing a flight on purpose is pretty dramatic. And I know drama."

"Yeah, I guess so," I say, carefully stirring the broth, which is starting to smell aromatic, more than the sum of its messy parts, maybe like me.

"You'll be glad to know that they canceled the flight anyway, so you just saved yourself a trip to the airport. You'll have to try for more drama next time. How about jumping out of a plane? Can I interest you in a misspelled tattoo?"

I shiver, not knowing what's scarier, needles, tattoos, or misspellings.

We talk for a few more minutes until I pull the matzah ball mixture out of the fridge. "Mom, thank you, but I need to go and finish what I started."

"If this boy is as special to you as I think he is, don't be afraid to tell him how you feel," my mom says. "A piece of advice, sweetie. In my life, I have many more regrets about things I didn't say than things I did. Fear and regret make cold bedfellows."

"Okay, Mom. Thanks, I think. Who said that? Shake-speare?"

"No! I made it up," my mom says. "Didn't it sound liter-ary? Methinks perhaps I should put it in a play. . . ."

"Bye, Mom." I chuckle, wishing I could hug her right then.

"Okay, Hannah. I love you. Take your time," she says be-fore hanging up.

I don't know whether she means to take my time with the soup or with Noah, but they are both on a timer at this point and any wrong move could ruin everything I'm trying to fix.

The only thing that looks worse than the matzah balls is how they feel, like wet mud mixed with soggy oatmeal. It doesn't smell great either.

"Faith. I need to have faith in the process," I say to myself, rolling the balls in my clean palms before gagging and then dropping them in the liquid one by one. Halfway through I realize I was supposed to strain the soup of all the solids first.

I run to get a small strainer but all I can find is a slotted spoon, so I slowly, carefully remove the vegetables a little at a time, trying to leave the matzah balls in the broth. While the veggies mostly floated, the matzah balls are sinking. They aren't fluffy like Noah's, but I hope they at least taste okay.

Finally, once the broth is mostly clear, I turn up the heat to boil again and hope against hope for the best. After some time has passed and the matzah balls at least seem fully cooked, I take the pot off the heat and start the process of bringing it upstairs to where Abe lives. Rather than disturb him, I gently place the pot in front of the door, take a pen out of my backpack, and tear a piece of paper from my notebook to leave a message.

I'm sorry you're sick.
I hope this makes you feel better.
Hannah

It's only a fraction of what I want to say to Abe, who has been nothing but kind to me, and only a decimal of what needs to be said to Noah, but now is clearly not the time. I did what I had to do, and now I need to go home empty-handed in all senses of the word.

Staring at the note, I frown. Rather than leave the inadequate note, I pick it up again and rip it up, putting the shreds of paper in my pocket to dispose of later. If Noah didn't answer my texts, that's probably the only answer I need. He'll most likely figure out I was the one who left the soup anyway. It's my way of groveling. No one else would make "I'm sorry" soup.

As I leave the building, I think I can hear someone open the apartment door, but I'm not sure if I imagined it or not. When I'm out on the street, I look up and don't see anyone in the window.

I text my grandmother, and she's there to pick me up in just a few minutes. The streets are empty. Everyone must be at church or at home celebrating with their families, which is how it should be.

When I get in the car with my grandmother, she hands me some coffee. "You look tired," she says. "Long day?"

"The longest," I reply. It's funny how much faster time went by when Noah and I worked together. Today I worked just as hard, if not harder, but it felt twelve times as long, especially as the day went on without any word from him.

The coffee is bitter and strong, much like my feelings about the day. I did a mitzvah, or a few really, without being asked or thanked, or even noticed. I just did them because they were the right things to do for someone who I care about, whether or not the feeling is still mutual. I can't regret feeding someone who's sick or taking care of their business so they could care for a loved one. But I have other things to regret that I can't seem to resolve.

"When is my next flight?" I ask my grandmother, blowing on my coffee. "I think I'm ready to go home."

"Tomorrow or the next day," she says. "Your mom is still working on it."

I nod. It doesn't matter anymore. Hanukkah is almost over, but there's always next year, or, as my mom said, we can just celebrate when I get home.

"Nana, I'm sorry there's been so much drama this week. Is there anything special you wanted to do for Christmas Eve? Anything at all?"

My grandmother smiles a little. "I don't mind the drama. It's been a long time since I've had a teenager. And in terms of the holiday, just spending Hanukkah with you is all I could want."

She pats my hand for a second, then puts her glove back on the steering wheel. We drive around looking at the Christmas lights on the way home. While my holiday is almost over and hers is just beginning, it seems fitting that we're sharing the lights all around us, a sign of hope, resilience, and, for me, dedication. While the story talks about rededicating the temple, maybe my miracle is rededicating myself to my family, to finding that common bond with my nana, and to sharing Hanukkah with her, something she hasn't celebrated since my grandfather passed away.

When we get home, I say the prayers over the candles, lighting all but one of them on the beautifully simple family menorah. "This is the best Hanukkah gift you could have given me. I'll light it every year and think of you and Grandpa Mel," I promise.

My grandmother squeezes my hand. "You know that your light shines brighter here than when you arrived. Don't let that light go out, no matter what," she says.

She turns on her Christmas tree lights, and we sit together on the couch and eat Blue Bell ice cream for dinner, too tired for much else, even to change out of my soup-splashed top. Considering how the week has gone, I'm pretty used to wearing food on my clothing, especially now when there's no one to judge me and nowhere to go.

I'm in the process of falling asleep on her shoulder when the dog starts barking like crazy. "Tell Elvis to tell Santa I'm Jewish," I say, pulling a blanket over me and curling up on the couch. "I'm going to sleep."

Too tired to climb into bed, I stay like that.

The dog keeps barking, and my grandmother stands up

to go over to the door with a flashlight. "I'm just going to see what he's barking at."

I grumble. "Last time he barked at a trash can. I'm sure it's nothing, but be careful," I say to my grandmother's back, then drop my head down, too tired to get up and investigate with her.

I'm pretty sure I'm already snoring, which I only do when I'm super tired, when she comes back in. The dog comes over and licks my face, but I swat him away until someone clears their throat near me. I push the dog a little, but the sound happens again.

I sit up and wipe away the drool, unclear if it's mine or the dog's as I finally open my eyes and rub them. Standing before me is Noah, in a button-down flannel, jeans, and sneakers, and his Astros hat. The circles under his eyes and his sunken cheeks are seriously pronounced. He looks almost as tired and messy as I do, although at least he isn't drooling.

"Hi," he says, his voice sounding more like a croak than usual, too.

"Hi," I echo, pulling the blanket over me for protection, but protection against what, I'm not sure.

"You're still here," he says as my grandmother stands up to quietly slip away with Elvis to the other room.

"Good night, Noah, Hannah." She kisses me on the fore-head and nods at him. That nod says more than words can. It says, "Don't mess with my granddaughter," or "Time to start groveling" with a side of "I hope you two can work it out."

For a moment after she leaves the room, neither of us says

anything. He just stands there as I sit on the couch clutching the blanket. Finally, I meet his eyes. "How's your grandfather?"

Noah seems to take it as an opening and sits down on the chair across from me. "He's got pneumonia. He's in the hospital for a couple of days, but he's going to be okay."

"I'm glad."

"Consuela told me what you did. Thanks for keeping the deli open and missing your flight. You didn't have to do that," he says, his eyes widening with something I'm having a hard time recognizing, until I look deeper. His eyes are full of hope. Hope that what I did meant something, I guess.

It did. It meant a lot to me, but it's not enough. I put myself out there for what? For him to pull away the second it got difficult.

Noah pastes on a smirk. "Your soup was interesting. I can't say I've ever had anything like it before. I hope you didn't serve it to the customers."

"Um, rude!" I say, throwing a pillow at him. He ducks and laughs.

I stick out my lip and pout. "It took hours! And you know it's hard for me to do anything I can't do well."

"Don't get me wrong, those matzah balls were perfect."

"See! I made perfect matzah balls," I say, sitting up a little.

"For baseball season. I mean, they were as hard and heavy as baseballs." Noah shakes his head and laughs again, but it's not funny to me. Tears well up in my eyes. I haven't cried in a long time, no matter how frustrated I've been, but now I can't stop. Nothing has turned out the way it was supposed to, especially Noah.

I wipe at my eyes and stand up with every intention of walking over to the door and opening it for him to exit, but I take two steps and trip over the blanket pooling at my feet, and soon I'm falling directly into his arms.

He reaches over and catches me, and I see the concern on his face. "I'm sorry. About everything. Your matzah balls do suck. That much is true. However, you, Hannah Levin, just forgot to add seltzer to make them fluffy. It's an amateur mistake. But I love that you tried."

He looks like he wants to say something else, but I steady myself and step out of the blanket.

"Well, it won't happen again. I don't see any matzah balls in my future, do you?"

"I don't know," Noah says, looking like there's a lot he doesn't know right now about my future, his future, and our future.

"But thank you for trying. It meant a lot to my grandfather. And to me," he admits, his eyes searching mine. "I'm sorry I didn't see that you called while we were in the hospital. I wasn't ignoring you. I was just worried about my grandfather, and then my phone died. I would never ignore you," he says, raising his voice a little when I don't say anything.

"No problem," I say lightly. "I wanted to help. I'm glad he's doing better."

"Me too," Noah says, "but I honestly don't know how much longer he can do this. Consuela and José will be home soon, so I guess we'll shut down until then and figure it out when they're back."

I can see from his pained expression how worried he is, but while my every instinct is to hug him and make him feel better, I know it would just make it harder for me to remember why we can't be together and make it that much harder to leave.

"Anyway, I'm sorry I joked about your matzah balls, but I kind of needed something to laugh at. You know, comic relief and all that. I didn't mean to insult you. I didn't want to hurt you at all."

"That's okay," I say. "I didn't intend to be so bossy about the deli."

"Yes, you did," he says. Noah gives me a small smile. It's not much, but I'm glad it's there on his face, a reminder of better days behind us and hopefully ahead for both of us, although separately.

"Maybe I did mean to be bossy, but it was because I care."

"I know." He leans over like he's unsure if he should hug me, kiss me, or what. Finally, he settles on a friendly kiss on the forehead.

"Take care, Hannah. If you're ever just visiting again, you know where to find me. If I don't find you first . . ."

His eyes flash once with a sad glance before he pastes on a resigned smile and leaves out the front door.

A second later, I run out to the porch to stop him, to tell him something, anything to make him stay, but it's too late. Elvis pushes his way out of my grandmother's room and barks at Noah's truck through the screen door until it leaves down the gravel driveway and can't be seen or heard anymore. Only then does the dog stop barking and turn to me like he's asking, "Now what?"

I sink back onto the couch alone until the dog jumps up and puts his head on my lap. "Now it's really over and I get ready to go home, Elvis," I say, scratching him behind the ears. He sighs like he's over the whole thing. "Same, buddy. Same."

16

I go upstairs to my room to pack for the third time. My grandmother has washed and folded some socks and pajamas I forgot and left them in a pile on top of the dresser, ready to go back to New York, to my regular life. Only, while New York is full of a lot of things, like reliable public transportation, restaurants, and parks, not to mention my friends and family, there's one major thing it's missing. It's missing Noah. He won't fit in my suitcase, even if he wanted to come back with me, which he's made clear he doesn't. Blum where you're planted is the beginning and the end of the conversation.

I reach for the ugly Hanukkah sweatshirt he gave me and the Blum & Sons T-shirt, now starting to get softer and a little stained from my cooking and serving attempts. But in spite of that, or maybe because of those imperfections, it's more precious to me, just like those torn Haggadahs we take out every year at Passover. Each drop of fading wine or horseradish is part of the story, just like my imperfect shirt is a testament to the time I've spent here and how I've grown.

A week ago, there's no way I would have worn either, but now they're not just outward symbols of how I've changed, they're memories of how much he pushed me to be a better person, to get out of my comfort zone to help others, to get to know my grandmother, and to give life outside New York a chance.

I roll the shirts and fit them in the corners of my suitcase, making room for them. I may be sad about how things ended, but I hope someday when the hurt is more of a distant ache that I'm grateful, too.

When almost everything is packed, I move the suitcase aside so I can curl up on the bed and try to sleep. Blum where you're planted, I repeat to myself as I try to doze off. But what if you're stuck like a weed? What if you've been planted in the wrong place?

I wake up however many hours later still in my clothes with the dog on the foot of the bed, his head on my suitcase.

I stretch out my arms and my neck, and he cries a little. "I don't know why you're so sad—you get to stay, and we've only known each other a week!" I tell the dog while I rub his belly. He seems placated for now, his tongue hanging out happily. A week was plenty of time for some of us to fall in love, including me and Elvis. For others, I guess no amount of time would be enough.

When I go downstairs with my furry companion trotting

behind me, my grandmother seems like she's in no rush. She's still in her plaid flannel pajamas, drinking coffee. Something seems off. "Shouldn't we be rushing out to take care of the horses? And getting ready for the trip to the airport?" I ask, pouring myself some coffee and trying to sip quickly, to fortify myself for the long trip, the one I was waiting for, then dreading, and now have finally come to terms with.

Like the last night of Hanukkah, it's bittersweet. I'm focused on both the happy holiday behind me and the sadness that it's almost over. The light will be brightest tonight, and then it will be gone.

"Has anyone ever told you that you worry too much?" my grandmother says with a twinkle in her eye over the lip of her mug.

"Only all the time," I say, sitting down in one of the wooden farmhouse chairs around the kitchen. "That doesn't mean I don't have good reason to worry."

"Have a kolache. Relax for a bit."

I take a pastry off the tray and bite into it, the sweetness overtaking my hesitation. If she's not worried about making it to the airport on time, maybe I shouldn't be either. I'm used to New York traffic, which takes forever. Maybe this attitude is a Texan thing. She knows more than I do about how long it takes to get everywhere.

"Why don't you go out to the barn?" my grandmother says once she's stood up and put our mugs in the sink and wiped a crumb off my cheek. "You may want to brush your hair, too."

I touch my curls, which do seem a little more out of control than usual, not that she's said anything over the past several days about the state of my hair or clothes. I chalk it up to just another weird thing about today, but I take her advice and spend five minutes putting myself together a bit more, putting my hair up in a ponytail, brushing my teeth, and even putting on a little lip gloss.

Once I'm feeling more or less human again, I go back downstairs, and my grandmother's dressed, too, and straightening up the living room.

I shrug but head toward the barn as suggested. Even before I get close, I sense a bunch of activity out there. The horses are making noise, the dog is back out there running around, and a figure is walking toward me quickly.

"Josh! What are you doing here?" I ask as he runs up and hugs me. "No wonder the horses are excited. They must remember you." He has a little stubble on his face and is wearing a Mets hat, but otherwise he smiles. "Seriously! How did you get here?"

He doesn't get a chance to answer any of my questions, though, because behind him come two more unexpected people, my parents, exiting the barn and heading right toward me with arms outstretched. They look wrinkled and tired but happy as I run toward them and they hug me tight like it's been forever since they've seen me. In a way it has since I feel like I've lived another life since I left the city.

"I know it's not the cool thing to say, but I really missed you, all of you," I say honestly once I let them go and take a look at all three of them to make sure I'm not imagining them here. "But I was heading to the airport soon. To come back to New York!"

My mom shrugged. "You're not the only one who can be dramatic. We thought we'd surprise you."

My dad puts an arm around me. He's back in a flannel shirt. My mom doesn't seem to mind as she beams at us both. "It's been too long since we've visited your grandmother and we thought, why not?"

The door to the front porch opens, and Nana makes her way across the lawn toward the barn with a big wave. She doesn't look surprised. No wonder she was in no rush this morning.

"How were the airports? How did you manage to get three seats?" All my questions tumble out until finally my mom answers with a laugh. "We didn't! We ended up driving."

Now the wrinkled clothes and stubble are making sense. "What? It must have taken forever."

"We took turns driving, kiddo," my dad says. "We did it in about thirty-eight hours, but that includes stopping a few times and staying over last night in Memphis."

"Wow . . . ," I say as it dawns on me that they made these plans before my flight was even canceled. Clearly my Nana knew all about it and helped arrange the surprise. "What about the LSAT?"

My brother smirks. "Luckily, I had an advanced tutor. I'm good to go."

I shoot him my own look, which means I want to hear more about the girl when my parents aren't around. Once my nana makes her way back inside, there are more hugs and questions about the trip and promises of coffee and kolaches for breakfast. If there's any tension between my parents and my grandmother, it's hard to tell. Everyone seems to be trying hard to be polite and focusing on small talk, but maybe it's the first step, just showing up for each other.

"So, slugger," my brother says when the adults are out of earshot. "What's going on with this Noah guy?" He says it lightly, but there's a little more to his voice, a protectiveness or something serious.

I make a face. "You know I hate to be called slugger. One bad dodgeball incident when I was nine! David Cohen's tooth was loose anyway. It was a baby tooth!"

"Not what I asked," Josh says.

I don't ask how he knows about Noah. It could be Tik-Tok, or my grandmother, or my parents, but it doesn't matter. "Nothing's going on. Anymore," I say, feeling the emptiness in my chest. "Why do you ask?"

Josh takes off his baseball hat and tries to smooth down his hair before giving up and putting the hat back on. "Who do you think talked us into coming? The dude is very persuasive, and he clearly cares about you a lot. There was even a Venn diagram and a slideshow."

A slideshow! He really did care, and he listened to my tips about how to advocate for himself. I smile and let myself hope for a fraction of a second before running my hand over my face as skepticism takes root. He said goodbye yesterday, or did he?

Josh walks toward the house, where my grandmother is

holding out his favorite mug. I, on the other hand, stand in the grass completely stunned. Noah called my parents two days ago and talked them into driving all the way across the country to be with me and to make amends with my grandmother.

My brother may think it's because Noah cares about me, and maybe it is, or maybe it's because he felt guilty that I spent my entire vacation helping him and his grandfather and he wanted to do something nice for me. Or maybe it was just Noah being spontaneous and coming up with yet another grand scheme without thinking too much about it in advance.

I mean, yeah, I'm really happy to see my parents and brother and to spend a little more time with my grandmother, but it doesn't really change anything between me and Noah.

The moment of hope I felt a second ago sinks down like a balloon being slowly inflated. If Noah had fallen in love with me the way I was falling in love with him, he probably would have told me himself. Granted, I never told him how I felt either, but now it's probably for the best anyway.

I let out a sigh and then walk toward the house to catch up with my family.

Night Eight of Hanukkah

We're playing an old game of Uno Josh found in the closet. "That's it—draw four, baby!" I say to my brother as he picks up more and more cards until he's holding at least half the deck.

"I think you're taking advantage of the fact that I'm too tired to strategize," he says with a yawn.

"There's no strategy, only luck, kind of like dreidel," I say. I start off with a grin, but it fades as I remember my last dreidel game with Noah, which ended up with us both winning. It's ironic, really, now that I feel like I've lost him completely. And worse, I've lost a little bit of myself in the process.

I thought I had everything figured out, and now I know that I don't. He cared enough to convince my family to come, but he doesn't care enough to call, text, or come by. I can't make sense of anything anymore.

I get up after putting my cards down, having won the game. "Listen, I'm starving," I say. "Anybody else?"

My grandmother gets up, too, and takes out a few dishes. "I thought I'd heat up a couple of casseroles," she says. "Maybe a salad, too? Nothing's open on Christmas Day, so I prepared ahead."

"Is that your famous mac and cheese?" Josh peeks into the fridge. My grandmother's mac and cheese is basically Velveeta, pasta, and cracker crumbs.

When their backs are turned, my mom rolls her eyes at my dad. Josh will eat anything that involves congealed cheese product, but my mom's much pickier.

"You know what would be great with that, Nana?" I say. "How about I whip up some latkes for the last night of Hanukkah?"

My dad chuckles. "No offense, Hannah, but the nearest fire station's about fifteen miles down the road and they're a volunteer crew. I'd hate to make them come out on Christmas."

I take out the potatoes and hold one out to him, shaking it for emphasis. "I'll have you know that I now know how to make perfect latkes. No fire extinguisher needed." I turn to the pan, put some oil in it, and bite my lip to stop myself from tearing up. Whether or not Noah is here, he's all around me, and it's clear he'll be hard to forget, no matter how hard I try.

I wipe at my eyes, hoping my family thinks the tears are caused by the onions I'm cutting and not the truth, because the whole truth is that I'm heartbroken. No, that's not it. Broken implies that something can be put back together. My heart was diced like these onions. It's decimated, not broken.

After shredding the potatoes, mixing them with the onions and spices as Noah taught me, I manage to fry them evenly just as planned. It helps to focus on what I can control. The heat, the oil, the timing. If this past week has taught me nothing else, timing is important. The latkes may not be as crispy or round as Noah's, but by the time I get them on the plate and on the kitchen table, my parents, brother, and grandmother are excited.

"Wow!" Josh says, spearing a latke with his fork, not waiting for anyone else to give him permission to eat. His brown eyes turn wide with the first bite, and he gives me a thumbs-up sign. "These are great, so much better than the frozen ones," he says, grabbing another.

My parents follow suit as my grandmother jumps up to find some sour cream and applesauce to serve with them. I first grab the sour cream but then put it down and reach for the applesauce. It's cloyingly sweet, but it reminds me of him, so I swallow it down anyway.

After everyone is done eating, I insist on cleaning up, too. My parents are so tired from the drive, it's the least I can do, especially since I'm the one who made the mess.

Oil is everywhere on the counter, on the cabinets, and on the stove.

I put the pan in the sink and pour some soapy water over it, washing away the oil and, in a way, just a little of my sadness.

I'm beginning to scrub the dishes when my mom comes up behind me and gives me a squeeze.

"They weren't that good," I joke with her, but don't turn because I'm not ready for her to see my face this sad.

"First off, they were excellent latkes," she says, turning me herself.

I glance down, but she puts a hand on my chin and I meet her eyes. "But the hug was because I'm proud of you."

"Thanks," I say, flicking her with a dish towel, "But anyone can follow a recipe, right?"

"That's not what I mean," my mom says. "I mean that you've been such a big help to your grandmother and to Noah and his grandfather and that you've really grown over the past week. At least the complaining stopped, and I heard you haven't been obsessing about college or stuck to your screens. It's been good for you, I can tell."

"It must be all those latkes and matzah balls," I try to deflect. "Lots of carbs. I'm probably growing in the wrong direction. . . ." I turn back to the sink to wash some more, but I can feel my mom's eyes on me, those all-knowing eyes that can always tell when I'm lying or withholding information.

She snorts but doesn't say anything. She doesn't have to because she knows that there's more to the story. Instead, she puts a hand on my shoulder so I look back at her. "Skipping your flight was choosing uncertainty, realizing that some plans need to be reformulated or scrapped altogether to make way for better things. To me that's growth. Control is overrated."

I hand her a dish towel to dry the plates in front of me.

"Thanks, Mom," I finally acknowledge. "Too bad growth hurts so much. It kinda sucks."

She just shakes her head. "That's why they call it growing pains."

We work in silence for a while, me washing the plates, her drying them and putting them away. Eventually the sun goes down, and I go into the living room expecting to curl up on the couch with my family and watch something on television, maybe one of the new Jewish Hallmark movies Abby and Becky keep texting me about.

It's about time there was some Jewish joy on television.

But instead, everyone seems to be getting up and putting on their shoes and jackets. "Where are you going?" I ask. "You just got here, so I'm assuming you're not leaving already."

Josh messes up my hair, not that it wasn't already messy. "Nope. We thought we'd go drive around town and see some lights or something."

"Maybe I'll stay here and hang out with the dog. You guys go on without me." I grab a blanket and wrap it around me on the couch. Sure enough, Elvis jumps up and snuggles right against me in the empty, warm spot Josh left.

"Slugger," Josh says, "we came here to hang out together. You're not getting out of this."

He pulls me up, and the blanket drops.

I shrug. I'd already looked at the lights a couple of times, but if that's what they want, I'm not going to argue. "Okay, fine. Just let me get ready." I run to the bathroom and take a few minutes to myself. It's almost like I forgot how loud and boisterous my family can be. It's been so quiet in this big house with just me and my grandmother, quiet enough that I've had too much time to think about Noah and everything. Maybe loud is exactly what I need to distract me.

I brush my teeth quickly and grab my own coat from the rack before looking down at my phone. No messages from Abby and Becky since the last text reminding me to watch the movie about the hot rabbinical student who moves to a small town. Apparently, Abby's moved on from lumberjacks to rabbis. I hope my friends aren't annoyed at me for missing our dinner and movie night, not to mention how I've been so ambivalent about our plans to go to college together. I'll have to make it up to them when I get back.

By the time I get to the rental car, everyone is already situated, my dad in the driver's seat, my grandmother up front with him, and my mom and Josh in the back seat of the SUV. When I slide in they immediately stop talking, which means they were probably talking about me. I stare at Josh, but he doesn't give anything away, just smirks. My mom is equally wide-eyed and innocent-looking.

"Fine," I say, stretching out my arms. "I was going to offer to sit in the middle, but I think I'll enjoy my comfy window seat so you can all continue talking about me." A few hours with my family and I'm back to being bratty, but they all laugh, so I guess it's okay to resume my regular role.

Josh groans but immediately starts chatting about taking the LSAT in January versus February and how he really wants to be done by spring break so he can enjoy himself. "I mean, if I do well in January, maybe Tamar and I can even go skiing in February," he says with a grin.

"Tamar's the study partner?" I ask.

Josh gets a dreamy look on his face, one I've never seen before in his many years of hanging out with a ton of girls. "Yeah. I can't wait for you all to meet her." He says it casually, but I can tell he means it. He's serious about this girl.

"Cool. I'll dig out all the naked baby pictures. You're absolutely fine with that, right? Oh, remember the one of him asleep in his Elmo diaper?"

He rolls his eyes as my mom giggles. It's getting dark in the car, but I swear that I can almost see a blush forming on Josh's cheeks, and he's not one to blush.

"If you'd been in the car with us, you would have heard about Tamar for thirty-eight hours," my mom teases. " 'Oh, I think Tamar likes this song. Did I tell you Tamar once went to Louisiana on a tikkun olam project to build houses . . . ? Tamar would love Dairy Queen,' and so on and so on."

"She sounds awesome," I say quietly. Once my mom starts chatting with my grandmother in the front seat, I turn to my brother. "How did you know she was the one?" I ask him, looking deep in his eyes for some wisdom, or something.

Josh grins but then shrugs. "I couldn't stop thinking about her and wanting to be around her. I even miss the annoying things about her."

"What could she possibly do that annoys you? I thought that was my job as your younger sister," I say, playing with my seat belt.

"Well," he says slowly. "She's always right, which is annoying, and she constantly points it out when I'm being lazy. And yet, it makes me want to try harder, so I guess it's a good thing."

"I like her already," I say, but my mind is already off Tamar and on to Noah, who pushes me out of my comfort zone, too, which ended up being a good thing, as my mom pointed out. I actually feel less anxious about things having to be perfect and fit into my ten-year plan now that I know some of the best things are unplanned anyway. Like the past week. I never saw it coming, and it was better that way.

I must have a wistful look because Josh elbows me.

"Did you tell him how you feel?" Josh asks.

I shake my head and look out the window at the lights on the gazebo where we had doughnuts with Sol, Irv, and Abe, and where we almost kissed. Then we pass by the big menorah, which is now glowing with all eight electric candles lit. It's so bright, but somehow seeing it makes me feel dimmer, without him.

"I don't want to talk about," I say, swallowing back tears as we continue to drive around the square past the deli, which is dark and empty. Not a surprise since nothing else is open either tonight.

The electric menorah in the window is fully lit, too, but something seems missing. Even Mordechai the Hanukkah gnome seems droopy now that the holiday is coming to an end. He now has to go back to the hall closet with the rest of the Hanukkah decorations, pushed aside until next year. "I know how you feel," I say under my breath.

"What did you say?" Josh asks.

"Nothing." I figure rambling about gnomes wouldn't make me feel any better, or change anything, other than make my family think I'm weird.

But when we finish going around the square for a second time, I start to get antsy and cramped in the back seat. "Um, can we go home now? I bet the horses need to be fed, and Elvis could use some food, too."

I don't tell them the truth, which is that all of the scenery may be pretty to them, but to me it's an overload of emotion. It's too much Noah, and I'm not ready.

My mom shoots my dad a meaningful glance when he turns toward her for a second before turning back to the steering wheel.

"There's just one more thing I want to see," he says, directing the car away from the square and in the opposite direction of my grandmother's house. I figure he wants to go see his old school or something else, so I just lean back and continue to look out the window with a groan. Some houses are covered in lights; some just have a simple wreath or an inflatable Santa on the lawn. I even see a blow-up Santa hanging from a window.

"That's gotta be traumatizing for kids." I nudge Josh. I don't even believe in Santa, and I don't want to see him in peril. About ten minutes later, I've seen enough, but my dad keeps driving closer to the older section of town, where the houses are closer to each other, unlike where my grandmother lives, which is mostly ranches and farms. The neighborhood is actually starting to look familiar, but I don't know why. Traffic is picking up, too.

"Hmm, I wonder what's going on? Maybe it's some sort of big family gathering or a church service," I say. "Why don't we head back?" I ask my dad, but my grandmother looks at me with a smile. She knows something. The quiet that falls over the car tells me that she's not the only one with knowledge as to where we're going.

18

"I think it's time," Josh says, pulling out a bandanna from his pocket and forming it into a blindfold.

"You're all being absolutely sus," I say, pushing his hand away.

"Sus?" my grandmother asks.

"Suspicious," Josh translates.

"I hate surprises, and being blindfolded means there's a surprise somewhere, or I'm being kidnapped by my own family. There better be a puppy involved. . . ."

"I thought you were done with having to have a plan," my mom says quietly.

"I need to have a plan to see where I'm going. That's pretty important," I grumble.

"Fine. Have it your way," Josh says, pouting a bit as my dad pulls into the parking lot of a church. At least that's what the building looks like in the dark. We all get out of the car, and my grandmother goes up the old cement stairs first.

I glance around the parking lot, and there are a decent number of cars. A light shines from a small window above the back door, but I can't see inside because the window is too high. My mom and dad go up the steps next, followed by Josh, who flashes me a relaxed grin. "Okay, I guess if you're smiling, we're probably not joining a cult or spending the night in jail," I say as I come up behind him.

"It's better than puppies," Josh says, opening the door with a flourish.

"Nothing is better than puppies. . . ." I groan before following him inside.

Once inside the building I hear voices, laughter, and music. So not a cult, or it's a happy one, at least. But then the music and all the noise suddenly stops and my entire family looks at me for my reaction. "What did I do? I don't even know where we are!"

With a big gesture, my grandmother opens the heavy metal door, the kind with a bar on it that you see in schools, but all I see is darkness at first. I can sort of make out bodies and hear whispers, but that's it. Until I see light flickering on the side of the room. Wait, it's not just lights. It's candles. Hanukkah candles. All eight of them for the last night of Hanukkah.

"Surprise!" a whole lot of people shout, and then the lights come on. I rub my eyes because the change in light levels is so dramatic I can't see anything at first. When I open them and focus again, I see Noah in the center of the room, beaming. He's next to a guy in a dreidel costume, who looks like the same one from the ice rink. It's not like there are probably a lot of dreidel guys in this part of Texas. This one is even wearing cowboy boots with his costume.

On his other side are Becky and Abby, who scream and run up to hug me.

"What are you doing here? Why haven't you texted me back!" I yelp at them.

"My dad had a ton of airline miles, so we thought we'd surprise you! We weren't sure we'd be able to get here, but we were lucky," Becky says as Abby points at her. "Someone thought you'd be able to tell if we were lying, so it was safer not to respond. Also, Noah kept us really busy in exchange for letting us stay with his parents."

Abby groans, but Becky laughs and says, "Don't listen to her; she loved it. How often do you get to hang out with college guys dressed like dreidels? Let's just say Eli has game. . . ."

I must look at Abby funny because she blushes. "What? He's a freshman, so he's only nineteen. I'm already eighteen."

"So no lumberjacks?" I ask.

"No lumberjacks need apply," Abby agrees.

"What do you mean, Noah kept you busy?" I ask, almost as an afterthought.

"He got our numbers and texted us to beg us to come. Then he made us work to get everything ready." Becky pouts.

"Yeah, good thing he's pretty cute," Abby says. "Because otherwise?"

I hug them both again and then look around the room, which seems to be a big all-purpose room in the church. There's Miss Kimberly with a few of her students, Sol, Irv, and Abe, Sol's cousin Leora Bernstein, and a couple of her friends we met at the senior center, and so many other familiar faces. My grandmother goes over to talk with Gillian and Nancy, my dad's talking to another guy who I think is Noah's dad, and my mom and Josh head straight for the doughnuts.

It's amazing, and I have an idea of how it all came together. Without saying a word, I wander toward the center of the room. That's when I realize that there's a big Star of David over the doorway, and a mezuzah on the doorframe that has been painted over.

"What is this place?" I ask Noah when he walks over to me. "I thought we pulled into a church's parking lot."

Noah pushes his hair out of his face, a nervous gesture I'm used to by now. "Well, you're half right. This is the current home of the Rosenblum Baptist Church, but you're also standing in what was Temple Shalom of Rosenblum. The Baptist congregation was nice enough to let us gather here tonight. And they even want to host some interfaith services this year, too. So that's cool."

"That's really nice, Noah," I say with a dry throat before going over to grab some punch and gulping it down and coming back to where he is. "It's a . . . great party. And not bad for someone who prefers to be spontaneous. I bet this took a lot of planning to pull off."

"I've planned this from the beginning. It's part of why I was so upset you were leaving early, and why I begged your parents and friends to help me throw a special Hanukkah party for you. I've been pretty busy, but I think it was worth it, don't you?"

I glance around at all the smiling faces, the elementary school students singing and dancing in a circle, the elderly folks clapping to the beat of the music. This isn't quiet or serious, and yet it's the most special Hanukkah I've ever had because it had to be carefully crafted. Nothing was taken for granted.

"Yes. It's worth it. You're worth it!" I glance up at him, my lip quivering as I wonder if he understands that all of it was worthwhile, even though we didn't work out.

Noah takes a step closer to me and holds out his hand as the music swells. It's not Hanukkah music, or holiday music. It's a love song from like a decade ago, but I barely notice. I take his hand without thinking, and he pulls me closer to him as we begin to sway.

Soon, other couples make their way to the dance floor, including my parents, Noah's parents, and even Abby with dreidel guy, now in regular street clothes, but I barely notice. I only have eyes for Noah.

"I saw the GoFundMe. I can't believe you managed to raise so much money online to save the deli so quickly. Thank you," he says, swallowing down his emotion, but he holds my hand tighter.

"It's amazing what you can do with the internet and a smartphone, Noah. You should try it," I joke, but blush at his gratitude.

The warmth permeates my hand, reminding me of the first time we danced together in the kitchen, when he tried to teach me how to two-step. My heart is heavy that this will be the last time, but I lean in closer to enjoy it.

I blush and look down at my sneakers. "I meant what I said in the video." I raise my eyes to look at him again. "The deli is a special place, and it deserves to be open. I'm glad I was able to help, and keep my end of the bargain," I confess with a bittersweet smile.

He nods. "You more than kept up the bargain," he says, holding me a little bit closer, like he doesn't want to let go either.

"You did, too, Noah. It's been a magical Hanukkah. Unlike any other."

"Well." Noah clears his throat. "I wanted to make it perfect for you."

"To give me something to remember?" I let out a sardonic chuckle. "I think you'd be hard to forget."

"No." Noah puts a hand on my face, and we're just inches apart. "I wanted to give you a reason to forgive me, and to come back for more than just a visit. I love you, Hannah. I'm sorry I've been such a—what did you call me? Chaos Monster? That I was such a mess that I wasn't able to see it or tell you how I feel."

"Chaos Muppet," I reply, then stand still, shocked at what he just said.

Noah puts his hands on my waist as mine make their way around his neck. "Is there any chance you feel the same way, or could feel the same way? Because if you do, we can find a way to work this out. I promise."

The tears start coming, and I'm pretty sure they are happy ones. "Yes, you nitwit. I've loved you ever since you made me latkes, or maybe back to the pickles. I don't know! It's been a while. And a lot of food was involved."

Noah laughs and leans his forehead against mine. "Why didn't you tell me? I could have saved some time tracking down Hanukkah gelt that doesn't have Santas on it, and I probably bought every blue and silver balloon in East Texas for tonight."

I wipe at my eyes. "I didn't think you felt the same way."

"How could I not love you?" he says, kissing me quickly, then looking deep into my misty eyes. "I love how grouchy you are without coffee, how much you care for kids, animals, and your family, although you pretend to be a grump that would put Moishe Oofnik to shame."

I open my mouth to protest, but he's still talking.

"I love how bossy you are, and how hard I have to work to impress you. But it's worth it to be the one who makes you smile. I want to earn those smiles. I also love that you push me to figure out my mess. Thanks to you, I talked my dad into letting me take a gap year to figure out what I want to study and how I'm going to balance college and the deli. Not going to lie, there were charts and numbers and a Google slideshow, but it worked. Oh, and my grandfather is going to make Consuela and José official partners in the business, so that will help, too. He said they may not be family by blood, but they're our mishpacha, part of our chosen family, and can help us carry on the legacy."

"That's awesome! I *am* impressed. And I'm smiling now," I say, but it's a slightly watery one until he wipes away a tear with his thumb and finds an eyelash.

"Make a wish," he says quietly as I lean up to him, close my eyes, and kiss him. It's soft and sweet, but it doesn't feel like a goodbye, or like most of the playful, frenzied kisses of the past several days. Rather, it's a new kind of kiss, one that is promising a new chapter for us.

However, hopefully this chapter doesn't involve making out in front of both sets of parents—especially since I haven't even officially met Noah's—my grandmother, and assorted senior citizens and elementary school children, so I break it off and he winks, holding out his hand for me to follow.

As he does, the YMCA song starts playing and a whole lot of people of different ages get onto the dance floor.

"Ugh! What is this music?" I ask, stopping and looking around.

Noah chuckles. "I ran out of time, so I put Eli in charge of the playlist. Pretty sure this is his bar mitzvah music. Just another reason to get out of here . . ."

"Yeah, before the Chicken Dance comes on. Or the

Electric Slide . . . There is nothing romantic about the Electric Slide."

We head out of the all-purpose room, down a hallway full of some old photos from Jewish events from the past and new photos of the Baptist congregation, but I don't stop to look closely because Noah has other things in mind.

He ducks into another room, and I follow him. It's some sort of library. The lights aren't on, so I follow Noah's voice to a couch inside. "How about we slide in here," he says in a low voice.

"Um, are you sure we should do this?" I ask.

"I may be getting better about planning," he answers, "but if there's still a time and place to be spontaneous, Hannah, then this is it."

"Good point," I say, making my way to the soft couch. "But how about the fact that we're making out in an old temple?"

Noah leans over and kisses me, making me melt like the grilled cheese he once made me on challah. I feel just as decadent, too, on the velvet couch where countless people have probably sat to discuss Torah and Sisterhood fundraisers.

"I'd say that since the temple had an active youth group once upon a time that these walls have seen plenty of Jewish teenagers hooking up. Maybe even our parents back in the day . . ."

"Gross! And now that portion of the evening is over," I say, sitting up and fixing my hair. But now I'm laughing and we're hand in hand back on the way to the party, just as it's supposed to be, especially as someone starts playing "Hava Nagila" over the speakers and Noah pulls me into the circle and we make our way around the room, filling the old temple with new joy, and bringing new life into what was once a lost community.

I'm smiling at Noah when I feel a tug on my other hand and it's my grandmother; then my dad breaks in next to her, my mom, my brother, and Abby and Becky. Soon, it's a chain of people I love, smiling and dancing, celebrating the Jewish community that was here and the one that we've managed to cobble together for one night to remind Rosenblum, and each other, that We Were Here. We Are Here. And if that's not the definition of A Great Miracle Happened Here, I don't know what is.

Epilogue: Five Weeks Later

I'm sitting on the couch watching Netflix with my parents and eating pizza after we've lit the Shabbat candles and said the prayers over the challah and wine. It's not the most exciting Friday night, but in six months, I'll be off to college, so I'm spending more time at home with my family while I can. I haven't heard from everywhere yet, so it's too soon to tell where I'm going, but I'm trying to embrace being without a plan—for now. I'm also thinking about widening my horizons, maybe even to Texas, which is starting to feel like a second home, and one I want to get to know better.

I grab the last slice of mushroom pizza, when the buzzer on our intercom goes off. "You didn't order anything else, did you?" I ask my dad, who looks guilty.

"Yeah, I was pretty hungry. You better let the delivery guy in," he says.

I jump up to ring the buzzer, but I don't hear anyone on the other end. A minute later, I can hear the elevator open and someone knocks on the door.

"Who is it?" I ask.

"Delivery," they answer.

I swing open the door and scream. It's Noah, holding a jar of pickles with a bow on it.

I immediately pull him inside the apartment and hug him. I just saw him last month since we ended up staying through New Year's, but it's like I saw him yesterday and haven't seen him in forever.

"Whoa! I don't want to drop the pickles."

"Good point! Don't drop the pickles or I'll have to call another delivery guy!" I take the jar, run to the kitchen counter, put it down, and then go directly back to Noah, where I give him a big kiss until one of my parents clears their throat and we break apart.

"What are you doing here?" I ask, now out of breath and blushing from my enthusiastic welcome that was maybe a little too PG-13 in front of my parents.

Noah drops his backpack on the floor. "Well, Sunday is Tu B'Shvat, and my Tu B'Shvat girlfriend was busy, so I thought I'd see if you wanted to go for a walk in Central Park and see some trees. . . ."

"So what next?" I ask. "Are you going to tell your Purim girlfriend about me?" I settle under his arm, which he wraps around me.

"I've already told her I'm only eating triangular cookies

with you. And I thought I'd book you for some upcoming holidays as well. Did you know there's a Jewish Valentine's Day called Tu B'Av? I need to do some research, but I'm hoping chocolate is involved."

Without another word, we walk out of the apartment into the city hand in hand as I try to come up with the perfect way to spontaneously celebrate together for a long time to come.

Once we're in Central Park, I drop his hand to go make a snowball and duck behind a tree to throw it at him. It lands right on his chest as he ducks down to make another one to throw at me.

"As a Texan, I don't know what this frozen white stuff is, but I know you're not escaping unscathed, Hannah," he says as I run toward a wide field where he follows and pulls me down until we're covered in snow on our backs staring at the sky above us. He leans over to kiss me as it starts to flurry right then.

"See? Magical," I say, kissing him back.

"Every day is a holiday with you, Hannah," Noah says, kissing me again. "So what next?" He grins in between trying to catch a snowflake in his mouth, then coughing. "It's much colder than it looks. And less fluffy."

He sits up and brushes off some of the snow, so I do the same but hold on to his hand.

"How about we plan to be spontaneous together?" I propose. "I'm thinking you, me, a Blum and Sons food truck traveling across the country this summer. Couldn't the fundraiser help make that happen?"

"That sounds like the perfect spontaneous plan, selling pickles and making memories. I like it," Noah says. "A lot."

"You can drive. As long as we stop for armadillos," I say, leaning over to kiss him one more time before heading off to our next adventure, together.

Acknowledgments

In many ways the seeds for this book were planted several years ago in multiple states. For several years I worked at the Museum of Jewish Heritage in New York City, which helped shape the way I thought about the meaning of Jewish community. However, even before I worked there, I went to the museum to see an exhibit called *Shalom, Y'All: Images of Jewish Life in the American South,* which fascinated me, as someone who grew up in the Northeast, where Jewish life seemed to have a different flavor and melody.

Later, I would marry a Texan and spend more and more time in Houston, where he grew up, as well as in small towns in East Texas, where my in-laws reside. On one such trip we saw an empty synagogue. The image stuck with me. While the people in this book and the setting are fictional, I tried to stay mostly true to the bold outline of the history of Jewish people in Texas. I recommend reading some of the excellent nonfiction books about the subject. While I also did my best to infuse the characters with personal beliefs filtered through my own lens as a Reform Jew, I want to acknowledge that there are different levels of observation and variations of religious practice within Judaism. My characters' understanding and practices may not be as traditional as more observant readers'.

I want to thank the following people who were instrumental in this book coming together.

First, my parents, who schlepped me to Hebrew school for years and even picked me up on time, mostly. I think it's safe to say Hebrew school officially paid off, at least more so than the baton twirling and knitting lessons. Thank you for always encouraging my reading and writing and for all those lively conversations around the dinner table.

In many ways, my dad was one of my first writing teachers. A published journalist, he used to sit for hours helping me type essays and papers on a real typewriter, which took a lot of patience for both of us. I also want to thank my mom for sharing her happy memories of when our family owned a Jewish deli in the Boston area many decades ago.

Suffice to say, this book wouldn't exist without my husband, Marcus, who drove all over Texas with me to visit old synagogues, cemeteries, and towns with Jewish history. He also makes really great latkes and taught me how to two-step, so that's a bonus.

Our daughter, Rebecca, while she prefers fantasy novels to romance, tried to help me avoid being too "cringe" in my use of slang. I hope I mostly succeeded and didn't embarrass her any more than usual.

Of course, I need to thank my amazing agents at McIntosh & Otis, Christa Heschke and Daniele Hunter. I'm so thankful for their encouragement, excellent editorial notes, and humor over the years.

I'm incredibly grateful to my editor, Wendy Loggia, who fell in love with the idea of this book from the start and helped bring the characters to life on the page. I'd like to also thank the entire Underlined/Delacorte Press dream team, including Alison Romig, Beverly Horowitz, Liz Dresner, Tamar Schwartz, Gillian Levinson, Abby Fritz, Becky Green, and Kimberly Langus. Of course, many of you may have picked up this book thanks to the extraordinary cover art by Farjana Yasmin, which is even more beautiful than I could have imagined.

The writing journey can be a solitary one, but I've been incredibly lucky to have many people who've made it far less lonely. First and foremost, Carrie DuBois Shaw. From coproducing theater in a deli on the Lower East Side to cowriting a Bigfoot-themed retelling of *Pride and Prejudice,* it's been quite the adventure. Thanks for always saying "Yes, and . . ."

Thank you as well to my book club gals, three of the smartest women I know: Sarah Richardson, Kimberly Small, and Jennifer Kikoler. Getting the book club back together has been one of the best parts of the past three years.

I'd also like to thank my former colleagues at the Museum of Jewish Heritage; my current colleagues at Purchase College, SUNY; my family in Boston, especially my aunt and cheerleader, Cindy Meola; the 2017 Debut group; JewishKidLit Mavens; Highlights Foundation; and many other writers, librarians, and booksellers I've met through various festivals, conferences, and events. A special thank you to Amy Giles for reading other projects and always giving awesome notes that help me be a better writer and storyteller.

If you didn't recognize it, I learned about the Chaos/Order Muppet theory from a 2012 *Slate* article by Dahlia Lithwick. For the record, I am absolutely an Order Muppet.

Finally, I want to thank our Texas friends and family for their inspiration, especially my mother-in-law, Patricia Aldredge, who raises horses and rescues any animal that is lucky enough to find her.

Shalom, y'all.

PAPERBACKS

LOOKING FOR YOUR NEXT ROMANCE? WE'VE GOT YOU COVERED.

Everything you want to read the way you want to read it.

GetUnderlined.com | @GetUnderlined

1496d